O. HENRY FOR THE HOLIDAYS

O. Henry
for the
Holidays

SEVEN
CLASSIC
THANKSGIVING
AND
CHRISTMAS
STORIES

LIBRARY OF AMERICA

Distributed to the trade in the United States
by Penguin Random House Inc.
and in Canada by Penguin Random House Canada Ltd.

The authorized representative in the EU for product safety
and compliance is eucomply OÜ, Pärnu mnt 139b-14,
11317 Tallinn, Estonia.
hello@eucompliancepartner.com

Library of Congress Control Number: 2025933455
ISBN 978-1-59853-833-5

1 3 5 7 9 10 8 6 4 2

Printed in the United States of America

CONTENTS

O. HENRY FOR THE HOLIDAYS

THE PURPLE DRESS

W E ARE to consider the shade known as purple. It is a color justly in repute among the sons and daughters of man. Emperors claim it for their especial dye. Good fellows everywhere seek to bring their noses to the genial hue that follows the commingling of the red and blue. We say of princes that they are born to the purple; and no doubt they are, for the colic tinges their faces with the royal tint equally with the snub-nosed countenance of a woodchopper's brat. All women love it—when it is the fashion.

And now purple is being worn. You notice it on the streets. Of course other colors are quite stylish as well—in fact, I saw a lovely thing the other day in olive green albatross, with a triple-lapped flounce skirt trimmed with insert squares of silk, and a draped fichu of lace opening over a shirred vest and double puff sleeves with a lace band holding two gathered frills—but you see lots of purple too. Oh, yes, you do; just take a walk down Twenty-third street any afternoon.

Therefore Maida—the girl with the big brown eyes and cinnamon-colored hair in the Bee-Hive

Store—said to Grace—the girl with the rhine-stone brooch and pepperment-pepsin flavor to her speech—"I'm going to have a purple dress—a tailor-made purple dress—for Thanksgiving."

"Oh, are you," said Grace, putting away some 7½ gloves into the 6¾ box. "Well, it's red for me. You see more red on Fifth avenue. And the men all seem to like it."

"I like purple best," said Maida. "And old Schle-gel has promised to make it for $8. It's going to be lovely. I'm going to have a plaited skirt and a blouse coat trimmed with a band of galloon under a white cloth collar with two rows of—"

"Sly boots!" said Grace with an educated wink.

"—soutache braid over a surpliced white vest; and a plaited basque and—"

"Sly boots—sly boots!" repeated Grace.

"—plaited gigot sleeves with a drawn velvet rib-bon over an inside cuff. What do you mean by saying that?"

"You think Mr. Ramsay likes purple. I heard him say yesterday he thought some of the dark shades of red were stunning."

"I don't care," said Maida. "I prefer purple, and them that don't like it can just take the other side of the street."

Which suggests the thought that after all, the fol-lowers of purple may be subject to slight delusions. Danger is near when a maiden thinks she can wear purple regardless of complexions and opinions;

and when Emperors think their purple robes will wear forever.

Maida had saved $18 after eight months of economy; and this had bought the goods for the purple dress and paid Schlegel $4 on the making of it. On the day before Thanksgiving she would have just enough to pay the remaining $4. And then for a holiday in a new dress—can earth offer anything more enchanting?

Old Bachman, the proprietor of the Bee-Hive Store, always gave a Thanksgiving dinner to his employees. On every one of the subsequent 364 days, excusing Sundays, he would remind them of the joys of the past banquet and the hopes of the coming ones, thus inciting them to increased enthusiasm in work. The dinner was given in the store on one of the long tables in the middle of the room. They tacked wrapping paper over the front windows; and the turkeys and other good things were brought in the back way from the restaurant on the corner. You will perceive that the Bee-Hive was not a fashionable department store, with escalators and pompadours. It was almost small enough to be called an emporium; and you could actually go in there and get waited on and walk out again. And always at the Thanksgiving dinners Mr. Ramsay—

Oh, bother! I should have mentioned Mr. Ramsay first of all. He is more important than purple or green, or even the red cranberry sauce.

Mr. Ramsay was the head clerk; and as far as I am

concerned I am for him. He never pinched the girls' arms when he passed them in dark corners of the store; and when he told them stories when business was dull and the girls giggled and said: "Oh, pshaw!" it wasn't G. Bernard they meant at all. Besides being a gentleman, Mr. Ramsay was queer and original in other ways. He was a health crank, and believed that people should never eat anything that was good for them. He was violently opposed to anybody being comfortable, and coming in out of snow storms, or wearing overshoes, or taking medicine, or coddling themselves in any way. Every one of the ten girls in the store had little pork-chop-and-fried-onion dreams every night of becoming Mrs. Ramsay. For, next year old Bachman was going to take him in for a partner. And each one of them knew that if she should catch him she would knock those cranky health notions of his sky high before the wedding cake indigestion was over.

Mr. Ramsay was master of ceremonies at the dinners. Always they had two Italians in to play a violin and harp and had a little dance in the store.

And here were two dresses being conceived to charm Ramsay—one purple and the other red. Of course, the other eight girls were going to have dresses too, but they didn't count. Very likely they'd wear some shirt-waist-and-black-skirt-affairs— nothing as resplendent as purple or red.

Grace had saved her money, too. She was going to buy her dress ready-made. "Oh, what's the use of bothering with a tailor—when you've got a figger it's easy to get a fit—the ready-made are intended for a perfect figger—except I have to have 'em all taken in at the waist—the average figger is so large waisted."

The night before Thanksgiving came. Maida hurried home, keen and bright with the thoughts of the blessed morrow. Her thoughts were of purple, but they were white themselves—the joyous enthusiasm of the young for the pleasures that youth must have or wither. She knew purple would become her, and—for the thousandth time she tried to assure herself that it was purple Mr. Ramsay said he liked and not red. She was going home first to get the $4 wrapped in a piece of tissue paper in the bottom drawer of her dresser, and then she was going to pay Schlegel and take the dress home herself.

Grace lived in the same house. She occupied the hall room above Maida's.

At home Maida found clamor and confusion. The landlady's tongue clattering sourly in the halls like a churn dasher dabbling in buttermilk. And then Grace came down to her room crying with eyes as red as any dress.

"She says I've got to get out," said Grace. "The old beast. Because I owe her $4. She's put my trunk in the hall and locked the door. I can't go anywhere else. I haven't got a cent of money."

"You had some yesterday," said Maida.

"I paid it on my dress," said Grace. "I thought she'd wait till next week for the rent."

Sniffle, sniffle, sob, sniffle.

Out came—out it had to come—Maida's $4.

"You blessed darling," cried Grace, now a rainbow instead of sunset. "I'll pay the mean old thing and then I'm going to try on my dress. I think it's heavenly. Come up and look at it. I'll pay the money back, a dollar a week—honest I will."

Thanksgiving.

The dinner was to be at noon. At a quarter to twelve Grace switched into Maida's room. Yes, she looked charming. Red was her color. Maida sat by the window in her old cheviot skirt and blue waist darning a st—. Oh, doing fancy work.

"Why, goodness me! ain't you dressed yet?" shrilled the red one. "How does it fit in the back? Don't you think these velvet tabs look awful swell? Why ain't you dressed, Maida?"

"My dress didn't get finished in time," said Maida. "I'm not going to the dinner."

"That's too bad. Why, I'm awful sorry Maida. Why don't you put on anything and come along— it's just the store folks, you know, and they won't mind."

"I was set on my purple," said Maida. "If I can't have it I won't go at all. Don't bother about me. Run along or you'll be late. You look awful nice in red."

At her window Maida sat through the long morning and past the time of the dinner at the store. In her mind she could hear the girls shrieking over a pull-bone, could hear old Bachman's roar over his own deeply-concealed jokes, could see the diamonds of fat Mrs. Bachman, who came to the store only on Thanksgiving days, could see Mr. Ramsay moving about alert, kindly, looking to the comfort of all.

At four in the afternoon, with an expressionless face and a lifeless air she slowly made her way to Schlegel's shop and told him she could not pay the $4 due on the dress.

"Gott!" cried Schlegel, angrily. "For what do you look so glum? Take him away. He is ready. Pay me some time. Haf I not seen you pass mine shop every day in two years? If I make clothes is it that I do not know how to read beoples because? You will pay me some time when you can. Take him away. He is made goot; and if you look bretty in him all right. So. Pay me when you can."

Maida breathed a millionth part of the thanks in her heart, and hurried away with her dress. As she left the shop a smart dash of rain struck upon her face. She smiled and did not feel it.

Ladies who shop in carriages, you do not understand. Girls whose wardrobes are charged to the old man's account, you cannot begin to comprehend— you could not understand why Maida did not feel the cold dash of the Thanksgiving rain.

At five o'clock she went out upon the street wearing her purple dress. The rain had increased, and it beat down upon her in a steady, wind-blown pour. People were scurrying home and to cars with close-held umbrellas and tight buttoned raincoats. Many of them turned their heads to marvel at this beautiful, serene, happy-eyed girl in the purple dress walking through the storm as though she were strolling in a garden under summer skies.

I say you do not understand it, ladies of the full purse and varied wardrobe. You do not know what it is to live with a perpetual longing for pretty things— to starve eight months in order to bring a purple dress and a holiday together. What difference if it rained, hailed, blew, snowed, cycloned?

Maida had no umbrella nor overshoes. She had her purple dress and she walked abroad. Let the elements do their worst. A starved heart must have one crumb during a year. The rain ran down and dripped from her fingers.

Some one turned a corner and blocked her way. She looked up into Mr. Ramsay's eyes, sparkling with admiration and interest.

"Why, Miss Maida," said he, "you look simply magnificent in your new dress. I was greatly disappointed not to see you at our dinner. And of all the girls I ever knew, you show the greatest sense and intelligence. There is nothing more healthful and invigorating than braving the weather as you are doing. May I walk with you?"

And Maida blushed and sneezed.

TWO THANKSGIVING DAY GENTLEMEN

THERE IS one day that is ours. There is one day when all we Americans who are not self-made go back to the old home to eat saleratus biscuits and marvel how much nearer to the porch the old pump looks than it use to. Bless the day. President Roosevelt gives it to us. We hear some talk of the Puritans, but don't just remember who they were. Bet we can lick 'em, anyhow, if they try to land again. Plymouth Rocks? Well, that sounds more familiar. Lots of us have had to come down to hens since the Turkey Trust got its work in. Bet somebody in Washington is leaking out advance information to 'em about these Thanksgiving proclamations.

The big city east of the cranberry bogs has made Thanksgiving Day an institution. The last Thursday in November is the only day in the year on which it recognizes the part of America lying across the ferries. It is the one day that is purely American. Yes, a day of celebration, exclusively American.

And now for the story which is to prove to you that we have traditions on this side of the ocean that are becoming older at a much rapider rate than those of England are—thanks to our git-up and enterprise.

Stuffy Pete took his seat on the third bench to the right as you enter Union Square from the east, at the walk opposite the fountain. Every Thanksgiving Day for nine years he had taken his seat there promptly at 1 o'clock. For every time he had done so things had happened to him—Charles Dickensy things that swelled his waistcoat above his heart, and equally on the other side.

But to-day Stuffy Pete's appearance at the annual trysting place seemed to have been rather the result of habit than of the yearly hunger which, as the philanthropists seem to think, afflicts the poor at such extended intervals.

Certainly Pete was not hungry. He had just come from a feast that had left him of his powers barely those of respiration and locomotion. His eyes were like two pale gooseberries firmly imbedded in a swollen and gravy-smeared mask of putty. His breath came in short wheezes; a senatorial roll of adipose tissue denied a fashionable set to his upturned coat collar. Buttons that had been sewed upon his clothes by kind Salvation fingers a week before flew like popcorn, strewing the earth around him. Ragged he was, with a split shirt front open to the wishbone; but the November breeze, carrying fine snowflakes, brought him only a grateful coolness. For Stuffy Pete was overcharged with the caloric produced by a super-bountiful dinner, beginning with oysters and ending with plum pudding, and including (it seemed to him) all the roast turkey and baked potatoes and chicken salad and squash pie and ice cream in the world. Wherefore he sat, gorged, and gazed upon the world with after-dinner contempt.

The meal had been an unexpected one. He was passing a red brick mansion near the beginning of Fifth avenue, in which lived two old ladies of ancient family and a reverence for traditions. They even denied the existence of New York, and believed that Thanksgiving Day was declared solely for Washington Square. One of their traditional habits was to station a servant at the postern gate with orders to admit the first hungry wayfarer that came along after the hour of noon had struck, and banquet him to a finish. Stuffy Pete happened to pass by on his way to the park, and the seneschals gathered him in and upheld the custom of the castle.

After Stuffy Pete had gazed straight before him for ten minutes he was conscious of a desire for a more varied field of vision. With a tremendous effort he moved his head slowly to the left. And then his eyes bulged out fearfully, and his breath ceased, and the rought-shod ends of his short legs wriggled and rustled on the gravel.

For the Old Gentleman was coming across Fourth avenue toward his bench.

Every Thanksgiving Day for nine years the Old Gentleman had come there and found Stuffy Pete on his bench. That was a thing that the Old Gentleman was trying to make a tradition of. Every Thanksgiving Day for nine years he had found Stuffy there, and had led him to a restaurant and watched him eat a big dinner. They do those things in England unconsciously. But this is a young country, and nine years is not so bad. The Old Gentleman was a staunch American patriot, and considered himself a pioneer in American tradition. In order to become picturesque we must keep on doing one thing for a long time without ever letting it get away from us. Something like collecting the weekly dimes in industrial insurance. Or cleaning the streets.

The Old Gentleman moved, straight and stately, toward the Institution that he was rearing. Truly, the annual feeding of Stuffy Pete was nothing national in its character, such as the Magna Charta or jam for breakfast was in England. But it was a step. It was almost feudal. It showed, at least, that a Custom was not impossible to New Y—ahem!—America.

The Old Gentleman was thin and tall and sixty. He was dressed all in black, and wore the old-fashioned kind of glasses that won't stay on your nose. His hair was whiter and thinner than it had been last year, and he seemed to make more use of his big, knobby cane with the crooked handle.

As his established benefactor came up Stuffy wheezed and shuddered like some woman's over-fat pug when a street dog bristles up at him. He would have flown, but all the skill of Santos-Dumont could not have separated him from his bench. Well had the myrmidons of the two old ladies done their work.

"Good morning," said the Old Gentleman. "I am glad to perceive that the vicissitudes of another year have spared you to move in health about the beautiful world. For that blessing alone this day of thanksgiving is well proclaimed to each of us. If you will come with me, my man, I will provide you with a dinner that should make your physical being accord with the mental."

That is what the Old Gentleman said every time. Every Thanksgiving Day for nine years. The words themselves almost formed an Institution. Nothing could be compared with them except the Declaration of Independence. Always before they had been music in Stuffy's ears. But now he looked up at the Old Gentleman's face with tearful agony in his own. The fine snow almost sizzled when it fell upon his perspiring brow. But the Old Gentleman shivered a little and turned his back to the wind.

Stuffy had always wondered why the Old Gentleman spoke his speech rather sadly. He did not know that it was because he was wishing every time that he had a son to succeed him. A son who would come there after he was gone—a son who would stand proud and strong before some subsequent Stuffy, and say: "In memory of my father." Then it would be an Institution.

But the Old Gentleman had no relatives. He lived in rented rooms in one of the decayed old family brownstone mansions in one of the quiet streets east of the park. In the winter he raised fuschias in a little conservatory the size of a steamer trunk. In the spring he walked in the Easter parade. In the summer he lived at a farmhouse in the New Jersey hills, and sat in a wicker armchair, speaking of a butterfly, the ornithoptera amphrisius, that he hoped to find some day. In the autumn he fed Stuffy a dinner. These were the Old Gentleman's occupations.

Stuffy Pete looked up at him for a half minute, stewing and helpless in his own self-pity. The Old Gentleman's eyes were bright with the giving-pleasure. His face was getting more lined each year, but his little black necktie was in as jaunty a bow as ever, and his linen was beautiful and white, and his gray mustache was curled carefully at the ends. And then Stuffy made a noise that sounded like peas bubbling in a pot. Speech was intended; and as the Old Gentleman had heard the sounds nine times before, he rightly construed them into Stuffy's old formula of acceptance.

"Thankee, sir. I'll go with ye, and much obliged. I'm very hungry, sir."

The coma of repletion had not prevented from entering Stuffy's mind the conviction that he was the basis of an Institution. His Thanksgiving appetite was not his own; it belonged by all the sacred rights of established custom, if not by the actual Statute of Limitations, to this kind old gentleman who had preempted it. True, America is free; but in order to establish tradition some one must be a repetend—a repeating decimal. The heroes are not all heroes of steel and gold. See one here that wielded only weapons of iron, badly silvered, and tin.

The Old Gentleman led his annual protégé southward to the restaurant, and to the table where the feast had always occurred. They were recognized.

"Here comes de old guy," said a waiter, "dat blows dat same bum to a meal every Thanksgiving."

The Old Gentleman sat across the table glowing like a smoked pearl at his corner-stone of future ancient Tradition. The waiters heaped the table with holiday food—and Stuffy, with a sigh that was mistaken for hunger's expression, raised knife and fork and carved for himself a crown of imperishable bay.

No more valiant hero ever fought his way through the ranks of an enemy. Turkey, chops, soups, vegetables, pies, disappeared before him as fast as they could be served. Gorged nearly to the uttermost when he entered the restaurant, the smell of food had almost caused him to lose his honor as a gentleman, but he rallied like a true knight. He saw the look of beneficent happiness on the Old Gentleman's face—a happier look than even the fuschias and the ornithoptera amphrisius had ever brought to it—and he had not the heart to see it wane.

In an hour Stuffy leaned back with a battle won.

"Thankee kindly, sir," he puffed like a leaky steam pipe; "thankee kindly for a hearty meal."

Then he arose heavily with glazed eyes and started toward the kitchen. A waiter turned him about like a top, and pointed him toward the door. The Old Gentleman carefully counted out $1.30 in silver change, leaving three nickels for the waiter.

They parted as they did each year at the door, the Old Gentleman going south, Stuffy north.

Around the first corner Stuffy turned, and stood for one minute. Then he seemed to puff out his rags as an owl puffs out his feathers, and fell to the sidewalk like a sunstricken horse.

When the ambulance came the young surgeon and the driver cursed softly at his weight. There was no smell of whiskey to justify a transfer to the patrol wagon, so Stuffy and his two dinners went to the hospital. There they stretched him on a bed and began to test him for strange diseases, with the hope of getting a chance at some problem with the bare steel.

And lo! an hour later another ambulance brought the Old Gentleman. And they laid him on another bed and spoke of appendicitis, for he looked good for the bill.

But pretty soon one of the young doctors met one of the young nurses whose eyes he liked, and stopped to chat with her about the cases.

"That nice old gentleman over there, now," he said, "you wouldn't think that was a case of almost starvation. Proud old family, I guess. He told me he hadn't eaten a thing for three days."

WHISTLING DICK'S
CHRISTMAS STOCKING

IT WAS with much caution that Whistling Dick slid back the door of the box-car, for Article 5716, City Ordinances, authorized (perhaps unconstitutionally) arrest on suspicion, and he was familiar of old with this ordinance. So, before climbing out, he surveyed the field with all the care of a good general.

He saw no change since his last visit to this big, alms-giving, long-suffering city of the South, the cold weather paradise of the tramps. The levee where his freight-car stood was pimpled with dark bulks of merchandise. The breeze reeked with the well-remembered, sickening smell of the old tarpaulins that covered bales and barrels. The dun river slipped along among the shipping with an oily gurgle. Far down toward Chalmette he could see the great bend in the stream outlined by the row of electric lights. Across the river Algiers lay, a long, irregular blot, made darker by the dawn which lightened the sky beyond. An industrious tug or two, coming for some early sailing ship, gave a few appalling toots, that seemed to be the signal for breaking day. The Italian luggers were creeping nearer their landing, laden with early vegetables and shellfish. A vague roar, subterranean in quality, from dray wheels and street cars, began to make itself heard and felt; and the ferryboats, the Mary Anns of water craft, stirred sullenly to their menial morning tasks.

Whistling Dick's red head popped suddenly back into the car. A sight too imposing and magnificent for his gaze had been added to the scene. A vast, incomparable policeman rounded a pile of rice sacks and stood within twenty yards of the car. The daily miracle of the dawn, now being performed above Algiers, received the flattering attention of this specimen of municipal official splendour. He gazed with unbiased dignity at the faintly glowing colours until, at last, he turned to them his broad back, as if convinced that legal interference was not needed, and the sunrise might proceed unchecked. So he turned his face to the rice bags, and, drawing a flat flask from an inside pocket, he placed it to his lips and regarded the firmament.

Whistling Dick, professional tramp, possessed a half-friendly acquaintance with this officer. They had met several times before on the levee at night, for the officer, himself a lover of music, had been attracted by the exquisite whistling of the shiftless vagabond. Still, he did not care, under the present circumstances, to renew the acquaintance. There is a difference between meeting a policeman upon a lonely wharf and whistling a few operatic airs with him, and being caught by him crawling out of a freight-car. So Dick waited, as even a New Orleans policeman must move on some time—perhaps it is a retributive law of nature—and before long "Big Fritz" majestically disappeared between the trains of cars.

Whistling Dick waited as long as his judgment advised, and then slid swiftly to the ground. Assuming as far as possible the air of an honest labourer who seeks his daily toil, he moved across the network of railway lines, with the intention of making his way by quiet Girod Street to a certain bench in Lafayette Square, where, according to appointment, he hoped to rejoin a pal known as "Slick," this adventurous pilgrim having preceded him by one day in a cattle-car into which a loose slat had enticed him.

As Whistling Dick picked his way where night still lingered among the big, reeking, musty warehouses, he gave way to the habit that had won for him his title. Subdued, yet clear, with each note as true and liquid as a bobolink's, his whistle tinkled about the dim, cold mountains of brick like drops of rain falling into a hidden pool. He followed an air, but it swam mistily into a swirling current of improvisation. You could cull out the trill of mountain brooks, the staccato of green rushes shivering above chilly lagoons, the pipe of sleepy birds.

Rounding a corner, the whistler collided with a mountain of blue and brass.

"So," observed the mountain calmly, "You are already pack. Und dere vill not pe frost before two veeks yet! Und you haf forgotten how to vistle. Dere was a valse note in dot last bar."

"Watcher know about it?" said Whistling Dick, with tentative familiarity; "you wit yer little Gherman-band nixcumrous chunes. Watcher know about music? Pick yer ears, and listen agin. Here's de way I whistled it—see?"

He puckered his lips, but the big policeman held up his hand.

"Shtop," he said, "und learn der right way. Und learn also dot a rolling shtone can't vistle for a cent."

Big Fritz's heavy moustache rounded into a circle, and from its depths came a sound deep and mellow as that from a flute. He repeated a few bars of the air the tramp had been whistling. The rendition was cold, but correct, and he emphasized the note he had taken exception to.

"Dot p is p natural, und not p vlat. Py der vay, you petter pe glad I meet you. Von hour later, und I vould half to put you in a gage to vistle mit der chail pirds. Der orders are to bull all der pums after sunrise."

"To which?"

"To bull der pums—eferybody mitout fisible means. Dirty days is der price, or fifteen tollars."

"Is dat straight, or a game you givin' me?"

"It's der pest tip you efer had. I gif it to you pecause I pelief you are not so bad as der rest. Und pecause you gan visl 'Der Freischütz' bezzer dan I myself gan. Don't run against any more bolicemans aroundt der corners, but go away vrom town a few tays. Goot-pye."

So Madame Orleans had at last grown weary of the strange and ruffled brood that came yearly to nestle beneath her charitable pinions.

After the big policeman had departed, Whistling Dick stood for an irresolute minute, feeling all the outraged indignation of a delinquent tenant who is ordered to vacate his premises. He had pictured to himself a day of dreamful ease when he should have joined his pal; a day of lounging on the wharf, munching the bananas and cocoanuts scattered in unloading the fruit steamers; and then a feast along the free-lunch counters from which the easy-going owners were too good-natured or too generous to drive him away, and afterward a pipe in one of the little flowery parks and a snooze in some shady corner of the wharf. But here was a stern order to exile, and one that he knew must be obeyed. So, with a wary eye open for the gleam of brass buttons, he began his retreat toward a rural refuge. A few days in the country need not necessarily prove disastrous. Beyond the possibility of a slight nip of frost, there was no formidable evil to be looked for.

However, it was with a depressed spirit that Whistling Dick passed the old French market on his chosen route down the river. For safety's sake he still presented to the world his portrayal of the part of the worthy artisan on his way to labour. A stall-keeper in the market, undeceived, hailed him by the generic name of his ilk, and "Jack" halted, taken by surprise. The vender, melted by this proof of his own acuteness, bestowed a foot of Frankfurter and half a loaf, and thus the problem of breakfast was solved.

When the streets, from topographical reasons, began to shun the river bank the exile mounted to the top of the levee, and on its well-trodden path pursued his way. The suburban eye regarded him with cold suspicion. Individuals reflected the stern spirit of the city's heartless edict. He missed the seclusion of the crowded town and the safety he could always find in the multitude.

At Chalmette, six miles upon his desultory way, there suddenly menaced him a vast and bewildering industry. A new port was being established; the dock was being built, compresses were going up; picks and shovels and barrows struck at him like serpents from every side. An arrogant foreman bore down upon him, estimating his muscles with the eye of a recruiting-sergeant. Brown men and black men all about him were toiling away. He fled in terror.

By noon he had reached the country of the plantations, the great, sad, silent levels bordering the mighty river. He overlooked fields of sugar-cane so vast that their farthest limits melted into the sky. The sugar-making season was well advanced, and the cutters were at work; the waggons creaked drearily after them; the Negro teamsters inspired the mules to greater speed with mellow and sonorous imprecations. Dark-green groves, blurred by the blue of distance, showed where the plantation-houses stood. The tall chimneys of the sugar-mills caught the eye miles distant, like lighthouses at sea.

At a certain point Whistling Dick's unerring nose caught the scent of frying fish. Like a pointer to a quail, he made his way down the levee side straight to the camp of a credulous and ancient fisherman, whom he charmed with song and story, so that he dined like an admiral, and then like a philosopher annihilated the worst three hours of the day by a nap under the trees.

When he awoke and again continued his hegira, a frosty sparkle in the air had succeeded the drowsy warmth of the day, and as this portent of a chilly night translated itself to the brain of Sir Peregrine, he lengthened his stride and bethought him of shelter. He travelled a road that faithfully followed the convolutions of the levee, running along its base, but whither he knew not. Bushes and rank grass crowded it to the wheel ruts, and out of this ambuscade the pests of the lowlands swarmed after him, humming a keen, vicious soprano. And as the night grew nearer, although colder, the whine of the mosquitoes became a greedy, petulant snarl that shut out all other sounds. To his right, against the heavens, he saw a green light moving, and, accompanying it, the masts and funnels of a big incoming steamer, moving as upon a screen at a magic-lantern show. And there were mysterious marshes at his left, out of which came queer gurgling cries and a choked croaking. The whistling vagrant struck up a merry warble to offset these melancholy influences, and it is likely that never before, since Pan himself jigged it on his reeds, had such sounds been heard in those depressing solitudes.

A distant clatter in the rear quickly developed into the swift beat of horses' hoofs, and Whistling Dick stepped aside into the dew-wet grass to clear the track. Turning his head, he saw approaching a fine team of stylish grays drawing a double surrey. A stout man with a white moustache occupied the front seat, giving all his attention to the rigid lines in his hands. Behind him sat a placid, middle-aged lady and a brilliant-looking girl hardly arrived at young ladyhood. The lap-robe had slipped partly from the knees of the gentleman driving, and Whistling Dick saw two stout canvas bags between his feet—bags such as, while loafing in cities, he had seen warily transferred between express waggons and bank doors. The remaining space in the vehicle was filled with parcels of various sizes and shapes.

As the surrey swept even with the sidetracked tramp, the bright-eyed girl, seized by some merry, madcap impulse, leaned out toward him with a sweet, dazzling smile, and cried, "Mer-ry Christmas!" in a shrill, plaintive treble.

Such a thing had not often happened to Whistling Dick, and he felt handicapped in devising the correct response. But lacking time for reflection, he let his instinct decide, and snatching off his battered derby, he rapidly extended it at arm's length, and drew it back with a continuous motion, and shouted a loud, but ceremonious, "Ah, there!" after the flying surrey.

The sudden movement of the girl had caused one of the parcels to become unwrapped, and something limp and black fell from it into the road. The tramp picked it up, and found it to be a new black silk stocking, long and fine and slender. It crunched crisply, and yet with a luxurious softness, between his fingers.

"Ther bloomin' little skeezicks!" said Whistling Dick, with a broad grin bisecting his freckled face. "W'ot d' yer think of dat, now! Mer-ry Chris-mus! Sounded like a cuckoo clock, dat 's what she did. Dem guys is swells, too, bet yer life, an' der old 'un stacks dem sacks of dough down under his trotters like dey was common as dried apples. Been shoppin' fer Chrismus, and de kid's lost one of her new socks w'ot she was goin' to hold up Santy wid. De bloomin' little skeezicks! Wit' her 'Mer-ry Chris-mus!' W'ot d' yer t'ink! Same as to say, 'Hello, Jack, how goes it?' and as swell as Fift' Av'noo, and as easy as a blowout in Cincinnat."

Whistling Dick folded the stocking carefully, and stuffed it into his pocket.

It was nearly two hours later when he came upon signs of habitation. The buildings of an extensive plantation were brought into view by a turn in the road. He easily selected the planter's residence in a large square building with two wings, with numerous good-sized, well-lighted windows, and broad verandas running around its full extent. It was set upon a smooth lawn, which was faintly lit by the far-reaching rays of the lamps within. A noble grove surrounded it, and old-fashioned shrubbery grew thickly about the walks and fences. The quarters of the hands and the mill buildings were situated at a distance in the rear.

The road was now enclosed on each side by a fence, and presently, as Whistling Dick drew nearer the houses, he suddenly stopped and sniffed the air.

"If dere ain't a hobo stew cookin' somewhere in dis immediate precinct," he said to himself, "me nose has quit tellin' de trut'."

Without hesitation he climbed the fence to windward. He found himself in an apparently disused lot, where piles of old bricks were stacked, and rejected, decaying lumber. In a corner he saw the faint glow of a fire that had become little more than a bed of living coals, and he thought he could see some dim human forms sitting or lying about it. He drew nearer, and by the light of a little blaze that suddenly flared up he saw plainly the fat figure of a ragged man in an old brown sweater and cap.

"Dat man," said Whistling Dick to himself softly, "is a dead ringer for Boston Harry. I'll try him wit de high sign."

He whistled one or two bars of a rag-time melody, and the air was immediately taken up, and then quickly ended with a peculiar run. The first whistler walked confidently up to the fire. The fat man looked up, and spake in a loud, asthmatic wheeze:

"Gents, the unexpected but welcome addition to our circle is Mr. Whistling Dick, an old friend of mine for whom I fully vouch. The waiter will lay another cover at once. Mr. W. D. will join us at supper, during which function he will enlighten us in regard to the circumstances that give us the pleasure of his company."

"Chewin' de stuffin' out 'n de dictionary, as usual, Boston," said Whistling Dick; "but t'anks all de same for de invitashun. I guess I finds meself here about de same way as yous guys. A cop gimme de tip dis mornin'. Yous workin' on dis farm?"

"A guest," said Boston sternly, "should n't never insult his entertainers until he 's filled up wid grub. 'T ain't good business sense. Workin'!—but I will restrain myself. We five—me, Deaf Pete, Blinky, Goggles, and Indiana Tom—got put on to this scheme of Noo Orleans to work visiting gentlemen upon her dirty streets, and we hit the road last evening just as the tender hues of twilight had flopped down upon the daisies and things. Blinky, pass the empty oyster-can at your left to the empty gentleman at your right."

For the next ten minutes the gang of roadsters paid their undivided attention to the supper. In an old five-gallon kerosene can they had cooked a stew of potatoes, meat, and onions, which they partook of from smaller cans they had found scattered about the vacant lot.

Whistling Dick had known Boston Harry of old, and knew him to be one of the shrewdest and most successful of his brotherhood. He looked like a prosperous stock-drover or a solid merchant from some country village. He was stout and hale, with a ruddy, always smoothly shaven face. His clothes were strong and neat, and he gave special attention to his decent-appearing shoes. During the past ten years he had acquired a reputation for working a larger number of successfully managed confidence games than any of his acquaintances, and he had not a day's work to be counted against him. It was rumoured among his associates that he had saved a considerable amount of money. The four other men were fair specimens of the slinking, ill-clad, noisome genus who carried their labels of "supicious" in plain view.

After the bottom of the large can had been scraped, and pipes lit at the coals, two of the men called Boston aside and spake with him lowly and mysteriously. He nodded decisively, and then said aloud to Whistling Dick:

"Listen, sonny, to some plain talky-talk. We five are on a lay. I 've guaranteed you to be square, and you 're to come in on the profits equal with the boys, and you 've got to help. Two hundred hands on this plantation are expecting to be paid a week's wages to-morrow morning. To-morrow's Christmas, and they want to lay off. Says the boss: 'Work from five to nine in the morning to get a train load of sugar off, and I'll pay every man cash down for the week and a day extra.' They say: 'Hooray for the boss! It goes.' He drives to Noo Orleans to-day, and fetches back the cold dollars. Two thousand and seventy-four fifty is the amount. I got the figures from a man who talks too much, who got 'em from the bookkeeper. The boss of this plantation thinks he's going to pay this wealth to the hands. He's got it down wrong; he's going to pay it to us. It's going to stay in the leisure class, where it belongs. Now, half of this haul goes to me, and the other half the rest of you may divide. Why the difference? I represent the brains. It's my scheme. Here's the way we're going to get it. There's some company at supper in the house, but they'll leave about nine. They've just happened in for an hour or so. If they don't go pretty soon, we'll work the scheme anyhow. We want all night to get away good with the dollars. They're heavy. About nine o'clock Deaf Pete and Blinky'll go down the road about a quarter beyond the house, and set fire to a big cane-field there that the cutters have n't touched yet. The wind's just right to have it roaring in two minutes. The alarm 'll be given, and every man Jack about the place will be down there in ten minutes, fighting fire. That 'll leave the money sacks and the women alone in the house for us to handle.

You 've heard cane burn? Well, there 's mighty few women can screech loud enough to be heard above its crackling. The thing 's dead safe. The only danger is in being caught before we can get far enough away with the money. Now, if you——"

"Boston," interrupted Whistling Dick, rising to his feet, "T'anks for de grub yous fellers has given me, but I 'll be movin' on now."

"What do you mean?" asked Boston, also rising.

"W'y, you can count me outer dis deal. You oughter know that. I 'm on de bum all right enough, but dat other t'ing don't go wit' me. Burglary is no good. I 'll say good night and many t'anks fer——"

Whistling Dick had moved away a few steps as he spoke, but he stopped very suddenly. Boston had covered him with a short revolver of roomy calibre.

"Take your seat," said the tramp leader. "I 'd feel mighty proud of myself if I let you go and spoil the game. You 'll stick right in this camp until we finish the job. The end of that brick pile is your limit. You go two inches beyond that, and I 'll have to shoot. Better take it easy, now."

"It 's my way of doin'," said Whistling Dick. "Easy goes. You can depress de muzzle of dat twelve-incher, and run 'er back on de trucks. I remains, as de newspapers says, 'in yer midst.'"

"All right," said Boston, lowering his piece, as the other returned and took his seat again on a projecting plank in a pile of timber. "Don't try to leave;

that 's all. I would n't miss this chance even if I had to shoot an old acquaintance to make it go. I don't want to hurt anybody specially, but this thousand dollars I 'm going to get will fix me for fair. I 'm going to drop the road, and start a saloon in a little town I know about. I 'm tired of being kicked around."

Boston Harry took from his pocket a cheap silver watch, and held it near the fire.

"It 's a quarter to nine," he said. "Pete, you and Blinky start. Go down the road past the house, and fire the cane in a dozen places. Then strike for the levee, and come back on it, instead of the road, so you won't meet anybody. By the time you get back the men will all be striking out for the fire, and we 'll break for the house and collar the dollars. Everybody cough up what matches he 's got."

The two surly tramps made a collection of all the matches in the party, Whistling Dick contributing his quota with propitiatory alacrity, and then they departed in the dim starlight in the direction of the road.

Of the three remaining vagrants, two, Goggles and Indiana Tom, reclined lazily upon convenient lumber and regarded Whistling Dick with undisguised disfavour. Boston, observing that the dissenting recruit was disposed to remain peaceably, relaxed a little of his vigilance. Whistling Dick arose presently and strolled leisurely up and down keeping carefully within the territory assigned him.

"Dis planter chap," he said, pausing before Boston Harry, "w'ot makes yer t'ink he's got de tin in de house wit''im?"

"I'm advised of the facts in the case," said Boston. "He drove to Noo Orleans and got it, I say, to-day. Want to change your mind now and come in?"

"Naw, I was just askin'. Wot kind o' team did de boss drive?"

"Pair of grays."

"Double surrey?"

"Yep."

"Women folks along?"

"Wife and kid. Say, what morning paper are you trying to pump news for?"

"I was just conversin' to pass de time away. I guess dat team passed me in de road dis evenin'. Dat's all."

As Whistling Dick put his hands into his pockets and continued his curtailed beat up and down by the fire, he felt the silk stocking he had picked up in the road.

"Ther bloomin' little skeezicks," he muttered, with a grin.

As he walked up and down he could see, through a sort of natural opening or lane among the trees, the planter's residence some seventy-five yards distant. The side of the house toward him exhibited spacious, well-lighted windows through which a soft radiance streamed, illuminating the broad veranda and some extent of the lawn beneath.

"What's that you said?" asked Boston, sharply.

"Oh, nuttin' 't all," said Whistling Dick, lounging carelessly, and kicking meditatively at a little stone on the ground.

"Just as easy," continued the warbling vagrant softly to himself, "an' sociable an' swell an' sassy, wit' her 'Mer-ry Chris-mus,' Wot d'yer t'ink, now!"

Dinner, two hours late, was being served in the Bellemeade plantation dining-room.

The dining-room and all its appurtenances spoke of an old regime that was here continued rather than suggested to the memory. The plate was rich to the extent that its age and quaintness alone saved it from being showy; there were interesting names signed in the corners of the pictures on the walls; the viands were of the kind that bring a shine into the eyes of gourmets. The service was swift, silent, lavish, as in the days when the waiters were assets like the plate. The names by which the planter's family and their visitors addressed one another were historic in the annals of two nations. Their manners and conversation had that most difficult kind of ease—the kind that still preserves punctilio. The planter himself seemed to be the dynamo that generated the larger portion of the gaiety and wit. The younger ones at the board found it more than difficult to turn back on him his guns of raillery and banter. It is true, the young men attempted to storm his works repeatedly, incited by the hope of gaining the approbation of their fair companions; but even when they sped a well-aimed shaft, the planter forced them to feel defeat by the tremendous discomfiting thunder of the laughter with which he accompanied his retorts. At the head of the table, serene, matronly, benevolent, reigned the mistress of the house, placing here and there the right smile, the right word, the encouraging glance.

The talk of the party was too desultory, too evanescent to follow, but at last they came to the subject of the tramp nuisance, one that had of late vexed the plantations for many miles around. The planter seized the occasion to direct his good-natured fire of raillery at the mistress, accusing her of encouraging the plague. "They swarm up and down the river every winter," he said. "They overrun New Orleans, and we catch the surplus, which is generally the worst part. And, a day or two ago, Madame New Orleans, suddenly discovering that she can't go shopping without brushing her skirts against great rows of the vagabonds sunning themselves on the banquettes, says to the police: 'Catch 'em all,' and the police catch a dozen or two, and the remaining three or four thousand overflow up and down the levees, and madame there"—pointing tragically with the carving-knife at her—"feeds them. They won't work; they defy my overseers, and they make friends with my dogs; and you, madame, feed them before my eyes, and intimidate me when I would interfere. Tell us, please, how many to-day did you thus incite to future laziness and depredation?"

"Six, I think," said madame, with a reflective smile; "but you know two of them offered to work, for you heard them yourself."

The planter's disconcerting laugh rang out again.

"Yes, at their own trades. And one was an artificial-flower maker, and the other a glass-blower. Oh, they were looking for work! Not a hand would they consent to lift to labour of any other kind."

"And another one," continued the soft-hearted mistress, "used quite good language. It was really extraordinary for one of his class. And he carried a watch. And had lived in Boston. I don't believe they are all bad. They have always seemed to me to rather lack development. I always look upon them as children with whom wisdom has remained at a standstill while whiskers have continued to grow. We passed one this evening as we were driving home who had a face as good as it was incompetent. He was whistling the intermezzo from 'Cavalleria' and blowing the spirit of Mascagni himself into it."

A bright-eyed young girl who sat at the left of the mistress leaned over, and said in a confidential undertone:

"I wonder, mamma, if that tramp we passed on the road found my stocking, and do you think he will hang it up to-night? Now I can hang up but one. Do you know why I wanted a new pair of silk stockings when I have plenty? Well, old Aunt Judy says, if you hang up two that have never been worn, Santa Claus will fill one with good things, and Monsieur Pambe will place in the other payment for all the words you have spoken—good or bad—on the day before Christmas. That 's why I 've been unusually nice and polite to everyone to-day. Monsieur Pambe, you know, is a witch gentleman; he——"

The words of the young girl were interrupted by a startling thing.

Like the wraith of some burned-out shooting star, a black streak came crashing through the window-pane and upon the table, where it shivered into fragments a dozen pieces of crystal and china ware, and then glanced between the heads of the guests to the wall, imprinting therein a deep, round indentation, at which, to-day, the visitor to Belle-meade marvels as he gazes upon it and listens to this tale as it is told.

The women screamed in many keys, and the men sprang to their feet, and would have laid their hands upon their swords had not the verities of chronology forbidden.

The planter was the first to act; he sprang to the intruding missile, and held it up to view.

"By Jupiter!" he cried. "A meteoric shower of hosiery! Has communication at last been established with Mars?"

"I should say—ahem!—Venus," ventured a young-gentleman visitor, looking hopefully for approbation toward the unresponsive young-lady visitors.

The planter held at arm's length the unceremonious visitor—a long dangling black stocking. "It's loaded," he announced.

As he spoke he reversed the stocking, holding it by the toe, and down from it dropped a roundish stone, wrapped about by a piece of yellowish paper. "Now for the first interstellar message of the century!" he cried; and nodding to the company, who had crowded about him, he adjusted his glasses with provoking deliberation, and examined it closely. When he finished, he had changed from the jolly host to the practical, decisive man of business. He immediately struck a bell, and said to the silent-footed mulatto man who responded: "Go and tell Mr. Wesley to get Reeves and Maurice and about ten stout hands they can rely upon, and come to the hall door at once. Tell him to have the men arm themselves, and bring plenty of ropes and plough lines. Tell him to hurry." And then he read aloud from the paper these words:

To the Gent of de Hous:
Dere is five tuff hoboes xcept meself in the vaken lot near de road war de old brick piles is. Dey got me stuck up wid a gun see and I taken dis means of comunikaten. 2 of der lads is gone down to set fire to de cain field below de hous and when yous fellers goes to turn de hoes on it de hole gang is goin to rob de hous of de money yoo gotto pay off wit say git a move on ye say de kid dropt dis sock in der rode tel her mery

crismus de same as she told me. Ketch de bums down de rode first and den sen a relefe core to get me out of soke youres truly,
WHISTLEN DICK.

There was some quiet, but rapid, manœuvring at Bellemeade during the ensuing half hour, which ended in five disgusted and sullen tramps being captured, and locked securely in an outhouse pending the coming of the morning and retribution. For another result, the visiting young gentlemen had secured the unqualified worship of the visiting young ladies by their distinguished and heroic conduct. For still another, behold Whistling Dick, the hero, seated at the planter's table, feasting upon viands his experience had never before included, and waited upon by admiring femininity in shapes of such beauty and "swellness" that even his ever-full mouth could scarcely prevent him from whistling. He was made to disclose in detail his adventure with the evil gang of Boston Harry, and how he cunningly wrote the note and wrapped it around the stone and placed it in the toe of the stocking, and, watching his chance, sent it silently, with a wonderful centrifugal momentum, like a comet, at one of the big lighted windows of the dining-room.

The planter vowed that the wanderer should wander no more; that his was a goodness and an honesty that should be rewarded, and that a debt of gratitude had been made that must be paid; for had he not saved them from a doubtless imminent loss, and maybe a greater calamity? He assured Whistling Dick that he might consider himself a charge upon the honour of Bellemeade; that a position suited to his powers would be found for him at once, and hinted that the way would be heartily smoothed for him to rise to as high places of emolument and trust as the plantation afforded.

But now, they said, he must be weary, and the immediate thing to consider was rest and sleep. So the mistress spoke to a servant, and Whistling Dick was conducted to a room in the wing of the house occupied by the servants. To this room, in a few minutes, was brought a portable tin bathtub filled with water, which was placed on a piece of oiled cloth upon the floor. There the vagrant was left to pass the night.

By the light of a candle he examined the room. A bed, with the covers neatly turned back, revealed snowy pillows and sheets. A worn, but clean, red carpet covered the floor. There was a dresser with a beveled mirror, a washstand with a flowered bowl and pitcher; the two or three chairs were softly upholstered. A little table held books, papers, and a day-old cluster of roses in a jar. There were towels on a rack and soap in a white dish.

Whistling Dick set his candle on a chair and placed his hat carefully under the table. After satisfying what we must suppose to have been his curiosity by a sober scrutiny, he removed his coat, folded it, and laid it upon the floor, near the wall, as far as possible from the unused bathtub. Taking his coat for a pillow, he stretched himself luxuriously upon the carpet.

When, on Christmas morning, the first streaks of dawn broke above the marshes, Whistling Dick awoke, and reached instinctively for his hat. Then he remembered that the skirts of Fortune had swept him into their folds on the night previous, and he went to the window and raised it, to let the fresh breath of the morning cool his brow and fix the yet dream-like memory of his good luck within his brain.

As he stood there, certain dread and ominous sounds pierced the fearful hollow of his ear.

The force of plantation workers, eager to complete the shortened task allotted to them, were all astir. The mighty din of the ogre Labour shook the earth, and the poor tattered and forever disguised Prince in search of his fortune held tight to the window-sill even in the enchanted castle, and trembled.

Already from the bosom of the mill came the thunder of rolling barrels of sugar, and (prison-like sounds) there was a great rattling of chains as the mules were harried with stimulant imprecations to their places by the waggon-tongues. A little vicious "dummy" engine, with a train of flat cars in tow, stewed and fumed on the plantation tap of the narrow-gauge railroad, and a toiling, hurrying, hallooing stream of workers were dimly seen in the half darkness loading the train with the weekly output of sugar. Here was a poem; an epic—nay, a tragedy— with work, the curse of the world, for its theme.

The December air was frosty, but the sweat broke out upon Whistling Dick's face. He thrust his head out of the window, and looked down. Fifteen feet below him, against the wall of the house, he could make out that a border of flowers grew, and by that token he overhung a bed of soft earth.

Softly as a burglar goes, he clambered out upon the sill, lowered himself until he hung by his hands alone, and then dropped safely. No one seemed to be about upon this side of the house. He dodged low, and skimmed swiftly across the yard to the low fence. It was an easy matter to vault this, for a terror urged him such as lifts the gazelle over the thorn bush when the lion pursues. A crash through the dew-drenched weeds on the roadside, a clutching, slippery rush up the grassy side of the levee to the footpath at the summit, and—he was free!

The east was blushing and brightening. The wind, himself a vagrant rover, saluted his brother upon the cheek. Some wild geese, high above, gave cry. A rabbit skipped along the path before him, free to turn to the right or to the left as his mood should send him. The river slid past, and certainly no one could tell the ultimate abiding place of its waters.

A small, ruffled, brown-breasted bird, sitting upon a dogwood sapling, began a soft, throaty, tender little piping in praise of the dew which entices foolish worms from their holes; but suddenly he stopped, and sat with his head turned sidewise, listening.

From the path along the levee there burst forth a jubilant, stirring, buoyant, thrilling whistle, loud and keen and clear as the cleanest notes of the piccolo. The soaring sound rippled and trilled and arpeggioed as the songs of wild birds do not; but it had a wild free grace that, in a way, reminded the small, brown bird of something familiar, but exactly what he could not tell. There was in it the bird call, or reveille, that all birds know; but a great waste of lavish, unmeaning things that art had added and arranged, besides, and that were quite puzzling and strange; and the little brown bird sat with his head on one side until the sound died away in the distance.

The little bird did not know that the part of that strange warbling that he understood was just what kept the warbler without his breakfast; but he knew very well that the part he did not understand did not concern him, so he gave a little flutter of his wings and swooped down like a brown bullet upon a big fat worm that was wriggling along the levee path.

A CHAPARRAL CHRISTMAS GIFT

THE ORIGINAL cause of the trouble was about twenty years in growing.

At the end of that time it was worth it.

Had you lived anywhere within fifty miles of Sundown Ranch you would have heard of it. It possessed a quantity of jet-black hair, a pair of extremely frank, deep-brown eyes and a laugh that rippled across the prairie like the sound of a hidden brook. The name of it was Rosita McMullen; and she was the daughter of old man McMullen of the Sundown Sheep Ranch.

There came riding on red roan steeds—or, to be more explicit, on a paint and a flea-bitten sorrel— two wooers. One was Madison Lane, and the other was the Frio Kid. But at that time they did not call him the Frio Kid, for he had not earned the honours of special nomenclature. His name was simply Johnny McRoy.

It must not be supposed that these two were the sum of the agreeable Rosita's admirers. The bronchos of a dozen others champed their bits at the long hitching rack of the Sundown Ranch. Many were the sheeps'-eyes that were cast in those savannas that did not belong to the flocks of Dan McMullen. But of all the cavaliers, Madison Lane and Johnny McRoy galloped far ahead, wherefore they are to be chronicled.

Madison Lane, a young cattleman from the Nueces country, won the race. He and Rosita were married one Christmas day. Armed, hilarious, vociferous, magnanimous, the cowmen and the sheepmen, laying aside their hereditary hatred, joined forces to celebrate the occasion.

Sundown Ranch was sonorous with the cracking of jokes and sixshooters, the shine of buckles and bright eyes, the outspoken congratulations of the herders of kine.

But while the wedding feast was at its liveliest there descended upon it Johnny McRoy, bitten by jealousy, like one possessed.

"I'll give you a Christmas present," he yelled, shrilly, at the door, with his .45 in his hand. Even then he had some reputation as an offhand shot.

His first bullet cut a neat underbit in Madison Lane's right ear. The barrel of his gun moved an inch. The next shot would have been the bride's had not Carson, a sheepman, possessed a mind with triggers somewhat well oiled and in repair. The guns of the wedding party had been hung, in their belts, upon nails in the wall when they sat at table, as a concession to good taste. But Carson, with great promptness, hurled his plate of roast venison and frijoles at McRoy, spoiling his aim. The second bullet, then, only shattered the white petals of a Spanish dagger flower suspended two feet above Rosita's head.

The guests spurned their chairs and jumped for their weapons. It was considered an improper act to shoot the bride and groom at a wedding. In about six seconds there were twenty or so bullets due to be whizzing in the direction of Mr. McRoy.

"I'll shoot better next time," yelled Johnny; "and there'll be a next time." He backed rapidly out the door.

Carson, the sheepman, spurred on to attempt further exploits by the success of his plate-throwing, was first to reach the door. McRoy's bullet from the darkness laid him low.

The cattlemen then swept out upon him, calling for vengeance, for, while the slaughter of a sheepman has not always lacked condonement, it was a decided misdemeanour in this instance. Carson was innocent; he was no accomplice at the matrimonial proceedings; nor had any one heard him quote the line "Christmas comes but once a year" to the guests.

But the sortie failed in its vengeance. McRoy was on his horse and away, shouting back curses and threats as he galloped into the concealing chaparral.

That night was the birthnight of the Frio Kid. He became the "bad man" of that portion of the State. The rejection of his suit by Miss McMullen turned him to a dangerous man. When officers went after him for the shooting of Carson, he killed two of them, and entered upon the life of an outlaw. He became a marvellous shot with either hand. He would turn up in towns and settlements, raise a quarrel at the slightest opportunity, pick off his man and laugh at the officers of the law. He was so cool, so deadly, so rapid, so inhumanly blood-thirsty that none but faint attempts were ever made to capture him. When he was at last shot and killed by a little one-armed Mexican who was nearly dead himself from fright, the Frio Kid had the deaths of eighteen men on his head. About half of these were killed in fair duels depending upon the quickness of the draw. The other half were men whom he assassinated from absolute wantonness and cruelty.

Many tales are told along the border of his impudent courage and daring. But he was not one of the breed of desperadoes who have seasons of generosity and even of softness. They say he never had mercy on the object of his anger. Yet at this and every Christmastide it is well to give each one credit, if it can be done, for whatever speck of good he may have possessed. If the Frio Kid ever did a kindly act or felt a throb of generosity in his heart it was once at such a time and season, and this is the way it happened.

One who has been crossed in love should never breathe the odour from the blossoms of the ratama tree. It stirs the memory to a dangerous degree.

One December in the Frio country there was a ratama tree in full bloom, for the winter had been as warm as springtime. That way rode the Frio Kid and his satellite and co-murderer, Mexican Frank. The kid reined in his mustang, and sat in his saddle, thoughtful and grim, with dangerously narrowing eyes. The rich, sweet scent touched him somewhere beneath his ice and iron.

"I don't know what I've been thinking about, Mex," he remarked in his usual mild drawl, "to have forgot all about a Christmas present I got to give. I'm going to ride over to-morrow night and shoot Madison Lane in his own house. He got my girl— Rosita would have had me if he hadn't cut into the game. I wonder why I happened to overlook it up to now?"

"Ah, shucks, Kid," said Mexican, "don't talk foolishness. You know you can't get within a mile of Mad Lane's house to-morrow night. I see old man Allen day before yesterday, and he says Mad is going to have Christmas doings at his house. You remember how you shot up the festivities when Mad was married, and about the threats you made? Don't you suppose Mad Lane'll kind of keep his eye open for a certain Mr. Kid? You plumb make me tired, Kid, with such remarks."

"I'm going," repeated the Frio Kid, without heat, "to go to Madison Lane's Christmas doings, and kill him. I ought to have done it a long time ago. Why, Mex, just two weeks ago I dreamed me and Rosita was married instead of her and him; and we was living in a house, and I could see her smiling at me, and—oh! h——l, Mex, he got her; and I'll get him—yes, sir, on Christmas Eve he got her, and then's when I'll get him."

"There's other ways of committing suicide," advised Mexican. "Why don't you go and surrender to the sheriff?"

"I'll get him," said the Kid.

Christmas Eve fell as balmy as April. Perhaps there was a hint of far-away frostiness in the air, but it tingled like seltzer, perfumed faintly with late prairie blossoms and the mesquite grass.

When night came the five or six rooms of the ranch-house were brightly lit. In one room was a Christmas tree, for the Lanes had a boy of three, and a dozen or more guests were expected from the nearer ranches.

At nightfall Madison Lane called aside Jim Belcher and three other cowboys employed on his ranch.

"Now, boys," said Lane, "keep your eyes open. Walk around the house and watch the road well. All of you know the 'Frio Kid,' as they call him now, and if you see him, open fire on him without asking any questions. I'm not afraid of his coming around, but Rosita is. She's been afraid he'd come in on us every Christmas since we were married."

The guests had arrived in buckboards and on horseback, and were making themselves comfortable inside.

The evening went along pleasantly. The guests

enjoyed and praised Rosita's excellent supper, and afterward the men scattered in groups about the rooms or on the broad "gallery," smoking and chatting.

The Christmas tree, of course, delighted the youngsters, and above all were they pleased when Santa Claus himself in magnificent white beard and furs appeared and began to distribute the toys.

"It's my papa," announced Billy Sampson, aged six. "I've seen him wear 'em before."

Berkly, a sheepman, an old friend of Lane, stopped Rosita as she was passing by him on the gallery, where he was sitting smoking.

"Well, Mrs. Lane," said he, "I suppose by this Christmas you've gotten over being afraid of that fellow McRoy, haven't you? Madison and I have talked about it, you know."

"Very nearly," said Rosita, smiling, "but I am still nervous sometimes. I shall never forget that awful time when he came so near to killing us."

"He's the most cold-hearted villain in the world," said Berkly. "The citizens all along the border ought to turn out and hunt him down like a wolf."

"He has committed awful crimes," said Rosita, "but—I—don't—know. I think there is a spot of good somewhere in everybody. He was not always bad—that I know."

Rosita turned into the hallway between the rooms. Santa Claus, in muffling whiskers and furs, was just coming through.

"I heard what you said through the window, Mrs. Lane," he said. "I was just going down in my pocket for a Christmas present for your husband. But I've left one for you, instead. It's in the room to your right."

"Oh, thank you, kind Santa Claus," said Rosita, brightly.

Rosita went into the room, while Santa Claus stepped into the cooler air of the yard.

She found no one in the room but Madison.

"Where is my present that Santa said he left for me in here?" she asked.

"Haven't seen anything in the way of a present," said her husband, laughing, "unless he could have meant me."

The next day Gabriel Radd, the foreman of the X O Ranch, dropped into the post-office at Loma Alta.

"Well, the Frio Kid's got his dose of lead at last," he remarked to the postmaster.

"That so? How'd it happen?"

"One of old Sanchez's Mexican sheep herders did it!—think of it! the Frio Kid killed by a sheep herder! The Greaser saw him riding along past his camp about twelve o'clock last night, and was so skeered that he up with a Winchester and let him have it. Funniest part of it was that the Kid was dressed all up with white Angora-skin whiskers and a regular Santy Claus rig-out from head to foot. Think of the Frio Kid playing Santy!"

CHRISTMAS BY INJUNCTION

C HEROKEE WAS the civic father of Yellow-hammer. Yellowhammer was a new mining town constructed mainly of canvas and undressed pine. Cherokee was a prospector. One day while his burro was eating quartz and pine burrs Cherokee turned up with his pick a nugget weighing thirty ounces. He staked his claim and then, being a man of breadth and hospitality, sent out invitations to his friends in three States to drop in and share his luck.

Not one of the invited guests sent regrets. They rolled in from the Gila country, from Salt River, from the Pecos, from Albuquerque and Phœnix and Santa Fé, and from the camps intervening.

When a thousand citizens had arrived and taken up claims they named the town Yellowhammer, appointed a vigilance committee, and presented Cherokee with a watch-chain made of nuggets.

Three hours after the presentation ceremonies Cherokee's claim played out. He had located a pocket instead of a vein. He abandoned it and staked others one by one. Luck had kissed her hand to him. Never afterward did he turn up enough dust in Yellowhammer to pay his bar bill. But his thousand invited guests were mostly prospering, and Cherokee smiled and congratulated them.

Yellowhammer was made up of men who took off their hats to a smiling loser; so they invited Cherokee to say what he wanted.

"Me?" said Cherokee, "oh, grubstakes will be about the thing. I reckon I'll prospect along up in the Mariposas. If I strike it up there I will most certainly let you all know about the facts. I never was any hand to hold out cards on my friends."

In May Cherokee packed his burro and turned its thoughtful, mouse-coloured forehead to the north. Many citizens escorted him to the undefined limits of Yellowhammer and bestowed upon him shouts of commendation and farewells. Five pocket flasks without an air bubble between contents and cork were forced upon him; and he was bidden to consider Yellowhammer in perpetual commission for his bed, bacon and eggs, and hot water for shaving in the event that luck did not see fit to warm her hands by his campfire in the Mariposas.

The name of the father of Yellowhammer was given him by the gold hunters in accordance with their popular system of nomenclature. It was not necessary for a citizen to exhibit his baptismal certificate in order to acquire a cognomen. A man's name was his personal property. For convenience in calling him up to the bar and in designating him among other blue-shirted bipeds, a temporary appellation, title, or epithet was conferred upon him by the public. Personal peculiarities formed the source of the majority of such informal baptisms. Many were easily dubbed geographically from the regions from which they confessed to have hailed. Some announced themselves to be "Thompsons," and "Adamses," and the like, with a brazenness and loudness that cast a cloud upon their titles. A few vaingloriously and shamelessly uncovered their proper and indisputable names. This was held to be unduly arrogant, and did not win popularity. One man who said he was Chesterton L. C. Belmont, and proved it by letters, was given till sundown to leave the town. Such names as "Shorty," "Bow-legs," "Texas," "Lazy Bill," "Thirsty Rogers," "Limping Riley," "The Judge," and "California Ed" were in favour. Cherokee derived his title from the fact that he claimed to have lived for a time with that tribe in the Indian Nation.

On the twentieth day of December Baldy, the mail rider, brought Yellowhammer a piece of news.

"What do I see in Albuquerque," said Baldy, to the patrons of the bar, "but Cherokee all embellished and festooned up like the Czar of Turkey, and lavishin' money in bulk. Him and me seen the elephant and the owl, and we had specimens of this seidlitz powder wine; and Cherokee he audits all the bills, C. O. D. His pockets looked like a pool table's after a fifteen-ball run."

"Cherokee must have struck pay ore," remarked

California Ed. "Well, he's white. I'm much obliged to him for his success."

"Seems like Cherokee would ramble down to Yellowhammer and see his friends," said another, slightly aggrieved. "But that's the way. Prosperity is the finest cure there is for lost forgetfulness."

"You wait," said Baldy; "I'm comin' to that. Cherokee strikes a three-foot vein up in the Mariposas that assays a trip to Europe to the ton, and he closes it out to a syndicate outfit for a hundred thousand hasty dollars in cash. Then he buys himself a baby sealskin overcoat and a red sleigh, and what do you think he takes it in his head to do next?"

"Chuck-a-luck," said Texas, whose ideas of recreation were the gamester's.

"Come and Kiss Me, Ma Honey," sang Shorty, who carried tintypes in his pocket and wore a red necktie while working on his claim.

"Bought a saloon?" suggested Thirsty Rogers.

"Cherokee took me to a room," continued Baldy, "and showed me. He's got that room full of drums and dolls and skates and bags of candy and jumping-jacks and toy lambs and whistles and such infantile truck. And what do you think he's goin' to do with them inefficacious knick-knacks? Don't surmise none—Cherokee told me. He's goin' to load 'em up in his red sleigh and—wait a minute, don't order no drinks yet—he's goin' to drive down here to Yellowhammer and give the kids—the kids of this here town—the biggest Christmas tree and the biggest cryin' doll and Little Giant Boys' Tool Chest blow-out that was ever seen west of Cape Hatteras."

Two minutes of absolute silence ticked away in the wake of Baldy's words. It was broken by the House, who, happily conceiving the moment to be ripe for extending hospitality, sent a dozen whisky glasses spinning down the bar, with the slower travelling bottle bringing up the rear.

"Didn't you tell him?" asked the miner called Trinidad.

"Well, no," answered Baldy, pensively; "I never exactly seen my way to.

"You see, Cherokee had this Christmas mess already bought and paid for; and he was all flattered up with self-esteem over his idea; and we had in a way flew the flume with that fizzy wine I speak of; so I never let on."

"I cannot refrain from a certain amount of surprise," said the Judge, as he hung his ivory-handled cane on the bar, "that our friend Cherokee should possess such an erroneous conception of—ah—his, as it were, own town."

"Oh, it ain't the eighth wonder of the terrestrial world," said Baldy. "Cherokee's been gone from Yellowhammer over seven months. Lots of things could happen in that time. How's he to know that there ain't a single kid in this town, and so far as emigration is concerned, none expected?"

"Come to think of it," remarked California Ed, "it's funny some ain't drifted in. Town ain't settled enough yet for to bring in the rubber-ring brigade, I reckon."

"To top off this Christmas-tree splurge of Cherokee's," went on Baldy, "he's goin' to give an imitation of Santa Claus. He's got a white wig and whiskers that disfigure him up exactly like the pictures of this William Cullen Longfellow in the books, and a red suit of fur-trimmed outside underwear, and eight-ounce gloves, and a stand-up, lay-down croshayed red cap. Ain't it a shame that a outfit like that can't get a chance to connect with a Annie and Willie's prayer layout?"

"When does Cherokee allow to come over with his truck?" inquired Trinidad.

"Mornin' before Christmas," said Baldy. "And he wants you folks to have a room fixed up and a tree hauled and ready. And such ladies to assist as can stop breathin' long enough to let it be a surprise for the kids."

The unblessed condition of Yellowhammer had been truly described. The voice of childhood had never gladdened its flimsy structures; the patter of restless little feet had never consecrated the one rugged highway between the two rows of tents and rough buildings. Later they would come. But now Yellowhammer was but a mountain camp, and nowhere in it were the roguish, expectant eyes, opening wide at dawn of the enchanting day; the eager, small hands to reach for Santa's bewildering hoard; the elated, childish voicings of the season's joy, such as the coming good things of the warm-hearted Cherokee deserved.

Of women there were five in Yellowhammer. The assayer's wife, the proprietress of the Lucky Strike Hotel, and a laundress whose washtub panned out an ounce of dust a day. These were the permanent feminines; the remaining two were the Spangler Sisters, Misses Fanchon and Erma, of the Transcontinental Comedy Company, then playing in repertoire at the (improvised) Empire Theatre. But of children there were none. Sometimes Miss Fanchon enacted with spirit and address the part of robustious childhood; but between her delineation and the visions of adolescence that the fancy offered as eligible recipients of Cherokee's holiday stores there seemed to be fixed a gulf.

Christmas would come on Thursday. On Tuesday morning Trinidad, instead of going to work, sought the Judge at the Lucky Strike Hotel.

"It'll be a disgrace to Yellowhammer," said Trinidad, "if it throws Cherokee down on his Christmas tree blowout. You might say that that man made this town. For one, I'm goin' to see what can be done to give Santa Claus a square deal."

"My co-operation," said the Judge, "would be gladly forthcoming. I am indebted to Cherokee for past favours. But, I do not see—I have heretofore regarded the absence of children rather as a luxury—but in this instance—still, I do not see——"

"Look at me," said Trinidad, "and you'll see old

Ways and Means with the fur on. I'm goin' to hitch up a team and rustle a load of kids for Cherokee's Santa Claus act, if I have to rob an orphan asylum."

"Eureka!" cried the Judge, enthusiastically.

"No, you didn't," said Trinidad, decidedly. "I found it myself. I learned about that Latin word at school."

"I will accompany you," declared the Judge, waving his cane. "Perhaps such eloquence and gift of language as I may possess will be of benefit in persuading our young friends to lend themselves to our project."

Within an hour Yellowhammer was acquainted with the scheme of Trinidad and the Judge, and approved it. Citizens who knew of families with off-spring within a forty-mile radius of Yellowhammer came forward and contributed their information. Trinidad made careful notes of all such, and then hastened to secure a vehicle and team.

The first stop scheduled was at a double log-house fifteen miles out from Yellowhammer. A man opened the door at Trinidad's hail, and then came down and leaned upon the rickety gate. The door-way was filled with a close mass of youngsters, some ragged, all full of curiosity and health.

"It's this way," explained Trinidad. "We're from Yellowhammer, and we come kidnappin' in a gentle kind of a way. One of our leading citizens is stung with the Santa Claus affliction, and he's due in town to-morrow with half the folderols that's painted red and made in Germany. The youngest kid we got in Yellowhammer packs a forty-five and a safety razor. Consequently we're mighty shy on anybody to say 'Oh' and 'Ah' when we light the candles on the Christmas tree. Now, partner, if you'll loan us a few kids we guarantee to return 'em safe and sound on Christmas Day. And they'll come back loaded down with a good time and Swiss Family Robinsons and cornucopias and red drums and similar testimonials. What do you say?"

"In other words," said the Judge, "we have discovered for the first time in our embryonic but progressive little city the inconveniences of the absence of adolescence. The season of the year having approximately arrived during which it is a custom to bestow frivolous but often appreciated gifts upon the young and tender——"

"I understand," said the parent, packing his pipe with a forefinger. "I guess I needn't detain you gentlemen. Me and the old woman have got seven kids, so to speak; and, runnin' my mind over the bunch, I don't appear to hit upon none that we could spare for you to take over to your doin's. The old woman has got some popcorn candy and rag dolls hid in the clothes chest, and we allow to give Christmas a little whirl of our own in a insignificant sort of style. No, I couldn't, with any degree of avidity, seem to fall in with the idea of lettin' none of 'em go. Thank you kindly, gentlemen."

Down the slope they drove and up another foothill

to the ranch-house of Wiley Wilson. Trinidad recited his appeal and the Judge boomed out his ponderous antiphony. Mrs. Wiley gathered her two rosy-cheeked youngsters close to her skirts and did not smile until she had seen Wiley laugh and shake his head. Again a refusal.

Trinidad and the Judge vainly exhausted more than half their list before twilight set in among the hills. They spent the night at a stage road hostelry, and set out again early the next morning. The wagon had not acquired a single passenger.

"It's creepin' upon my faculties," remarked Trinidad, "that borrowin' kids at Christmas is somethin' like tryin' to steal butter from a man that's got hot pancakes a-comin'."

"It is undoubtedly an indisputable fact," said the Judge, "that the—ah—family ties seem to be more coherent and assertive at that period of the year."

On the day before Christmas they drove thirty miles, making four fruitless halts and appeals. Everywhere they found "kids" at a premium.

The sun was low when the wife of a section boss on a lonely railroad huddled her unavailable progeny behind her and said:

"There's a woman that's just took charge of the railroad eatin' house down at Granite Junction. I hear she's got a little boy. Maybe she might let him go."

Trinidad pulled up his mules at Granite Junction at five o'clock in the afternoon. The train had just departed with its load of fed and appeased passengers.

On the steps of the eating house they found a thin and glowering boy of ten smoking a cigarette. The dining-room had been left in chaos by the peripatetic appetites. A youngish woman reclined, exhausted, in a chair. Her face wore sharp lines of worry. She had once possessed a certain style of beauty that would never wholly leave her and would never wholly return. Trinidad set forth his mission.

"I'd count it a mercy if you'd take Bobby for a while," she said, wearily. "I'm on the go from morning till night, and I don't have time to 'tend to him. He's learning bad habits from the men. It'll be the only chance he'll have to get any Christmas."

The men went outside and conferred with Bobby. Trinidad pictured the glories of the Christmas tree and presents in lively colours.

"And, moreover, my young friend," added the Judge, "Santa Claus himself will personally distribute the offerings that will typify the gifts conveyed by the shepherds of Bethlehem to——"

"Aw, come off," said the boy, squinting his small eyes. "I ain't no kid. There ain't any Santa Claus. It's your folks that buys toys and sneaks 'em in when you're asleep. And they make marks in the soot in the chimney with the tongs to look like Santa's sleigh tracks."

"That might be so," argued Trinidad, "but Christmas trees ain't no fairy tale. This one's goin' to look like the ten-cent store in Albuquerque, all strung up in a redwood. There's tops and drums and Noah's arks and——"

"Oh, rats!" said Bobby, wearily. "I cut them out long ago. I'd like to have a rifle—not a target one—a real one, to shoot wildcats with; but I guess you won't have any of them on your old tree."

"Well, I can't say for sure," said Trinidad diplomatically; "it might be. You go along with us and see."

The hope thus held out, though faint, won the boy's hesitating consent to go. With this solitary beneficiary for Cherokee's holiday bounty, the canvassers spun along the homeward road.

In Yellowhammer the empty storeroom had been transformed into what might have passed as the bower of an Arizona fairy. The ladies had done their work well. A tall Christmas tree, covered to the topmost branch with candles, spangles, and toys sufficient for more than a score of children, stood in the centre of the floor. Near sunset anxious eyes had begun to scan the street for the returning team of the child-providers. At noon that day Cherokee had dashed into town with his new sleigh piled high with bundles and boxes and bales of all sizes and shapes. So intent was he upon the arrangements for his altruistic plans that the dearth of childhood did not receive his notice. No one gave away the humiliating state of Yellowhammer, for the efforts of

Trinidad and the Judge were expected to supply the deficiency.

When the sun went down Cherokee, with many winks and arch grins on his seasoned face, went into retirement with the bundle containing the Santa Claus raiment and a pack containing special and undisclosed gifts.

"When the kids are rounded up," he instructed the volunteer arrangement committee, "light up the candles on the tree and set 'em to playin' 'Pussy Wants a Corner' and 'King William.' When they get good and at it, why—old Santa'll slide in the door. I reckon there'll be plenty of gifts to go 'round."

The ladies were flitting about the tree, giving it final touches that were never final. The Spangler Sisters were there in costume as Lady Violet de Vere and Marie, the maid, in their new drama, "The Miner's Bride." The theatre did not open until nine, and they were welcome assistants of the Christmas tree committee. Every minute heads would pop out the door to look and listen for the approach of Trinidad's team. And now this became an anxious function, for night had fallen and it would soon be necessary to light the candles on the tree, and Cherokee was apt to make an irruption at any time in his Kriss Kringle garb.

At length the wagon of the child "rustlers" rattled down the street to the door. The ladies, with little screams of excitement, flew to the lighting of the candles. The men of Yellowhammer passed in and out restlessly or stood about the room in embarrassed groups.

Trinidad and the Judge, bearing the marks of protracted travel, entered, conducting between them a single impish boy, who stared with sullen, pessimistic eyes at the gaudy tree.

"Where are the other children?" asked the assayer's wife, the acknowledged leader of all social functions.

"Ma'am," said Trinidad with a sigh, "prospectin' for kids at Christmas time is like huntin' in limestone for silver. This parental business is one that I haven't no chance to comprehend. It seems that fathers and mothers are willin' for their offsprings to be drownded, stole, fed on poison oak, and et by catamounts 364 days in the year; but on Christmas Day they insists on enjoyin' the exclusive mortification of their company. This here young biped, ma'am, is all that washes out of our two days' manœuvres."

"Oh, the sweet little boy!" cooed Miss Erma, trailing her De Vere robes to centre of stage.

"Aw, shut up," said Bobby, with a scowl. "Who's a kid? You ain't, you bet."

"Fresh brat!" breathed Miss Erma, beneath her enamelled smile.

"We done the best we could," said Trinidad. "It's tough on Cherokee, but it can't be helped."

Then the door opened and Cherokee entered in

the conventional dress of Saint Nick. A white rippling beard and flowing hair covered his face almost
to his dark and shining eyes. Over his shoulder he
carried a pack.

No one stirred as he came in. Even the Spangler
Sisters ceased their coquettish poses and stared
curiously at the tall figure. Bobby stood with his
hands in his pockets gazing gloomily at the effemi-
nate and childish tree. Cherokee put down his pack
and looked wonderingly about the room. Perhaps
he fancied that a bevy of eager children were being
herded somewhere, to be loosed upon his entrance.
He went up to Bobby and extended his red-mittened
hand.

"Merry Christmas, little boy," said Cherokee.
"Anything on the tree you want they'll get it down
for you. Won't you shake hands with Santa Claus?"

"There ain't any Santa Claus," whined the boy.
"You've got old false billy goat's whiskers on your
face. I ain't no kid. What do I want with dolls and
tin horses? The driver said you'd have a rifle, and you
haven't. I want to go home."

Trinidad stepped into the breach. He shook
Cherokee's hand in warm greeting.

"I'm sorry, Cherokee," he explained. "There
never was a kid in Yellowhammer. We tried to rustle a bunch of 'em for your swaree, but this sardine
was all we could catch. He's a atheist, and he don't
believe in Santa Claus. It's a shame for you to be

out all this truck. But me and the Judge was sure we could round up a wagonful of candidates for your gimcracks."

"That's all right," said Cherokee gravely. "The expense don't amount to nothin' worth mentionin'. We can dump the stuff down a shaft or throw it away. I don't know what I was thinkin' about; but it never occurred to my cogitations that there wasn't any kids in Yellowhammer."

Meanwhile the company had relaxed into a hollow but praiseworthy imitation of a pleasure gathering.

Bobby had retreated to a distant chair, and was coldly regarding the scene with ennui plastered thick upon him. Cherokee, lingering with his original idea, went over and sat beside him.

"Where do you live, little boy?" he asked respectfully.

"Granite Junction," said Bobby without emphasis.

The room was warm. Cherokee took off his cap, and then removed his beard and wig.

"Say!" exclaimed Bobby, with a show of interest, "I know your mug, all right."

"Did you ever see me before?" asked Cherokee.

"I don't know; but I've seen your picture lots of times."

"Where?"

The boy hesitated. "On the bureau at home," he answered.

"Let's have your name, if you please, buddy."

"Robert Lumsden. The picture belongs to my mother. She puts it under her pillow of nights. And once I saw her kiss it. I wouldn't. But women are that way."

Cherokee rose and beckoned to Trinidad.

"Keep this boy by you till I come back," he said. "I'm goin' to shed these Christmas duds, and hitch up my sleigh. I'm goin' to take this kid home."

"Well, infidel," said Trinidad, taking Cherokee's vacant chair, "and so you are too superannuated and effete to yearn for such mockeries as candy and toys, it seems."

"I don't like you," said Bobby, with acrimony. "You said there would be a rifle. A fellow can't even smoke. I wish I was at home."

Cherokee drove his sleigh to the door, and they lifted Bobby in beside him. The team of fine horses sprang away prancingly over the hard snow. Cherokee had on his $500 overcoat of baby sealskin. The laprobe that he drew about them was as warm as velvet.

Bobby slipped a cigarette from his pocket and was trying to snap a match.

"Throw that cigarette away," said Cherokee, in a quiet but new voice.

Bobby hesitated, and then dropped the cylinder overboard.

"Throw the box, too," commanded the new voice.

More reluctantly the boy obeyed.

"Say," said Bobby, presently, "I like you. I don't know why. Nobody never made me do anything I didn't want to do before."

"Tell me, kid," said Cherokee, not using his new voice, "are you sure your mother kissed that picture that looks like me?"

"Dead sure. I seen her do it."

"Didn't you remark somethin' a while ago about wanting a rifle?"

"You bet I did. Will you get me one?"

"To-morrow—silver-mounted."

Cherokee took out his watch.

"Half-past nine. We'll hit the Junction plumb on time with Christmas Day. Are you cold? Sit closer, son."

THE GIFT OF THE MAGI

ONE DOLLAR and eighty-seven cents. That was all. And sixty cents of it was in pennies. Pennies saved one and two at a time by bulldozing the grocer and the vegetable man and the butcher until one's cheeks burned with the silent imputation of parsimony that such close dealing implied. Three times Della counted it. One dollar and eighty-seven cents. And the next day would be Christmas.

There was clearly nothing to do but flop down on the shabby little couch and howl. So Della did it. Which instigates the moral reflection that life is made up of sobs, sniffles, and smiles, with sniffles predominating.

While the mistress of the home is gradually subsiding from the first stage to the second, take a look at the home. A furnished flat at $8 per week. It did not exactly beggar description, but it certainly had that word on the lookout for the mendicancy squad.

In the vestibule below was a letter-box into which no letter would go, and an electric button from which no mortal finger could coax a ring. Also appertaining thereunto was a card bearing the name "Mr. James Dillingham Young."

The "Dillingham" had been flung to the breeze during a former period of prosperity when its possessor was being paid $30 per week. Now, when the income was shrunk to $20, the letters of "Dillingham" looked blurred, as though they were thinking seriously of contracting to a modest and unassuming D. But whenever Mr. James Dillingham Young came home and reached his flat above he was called "Jim" and greatly hugged by Mrs. James Dillingham Young, already introduced to you as Della. Which is all very good.

Della finished her cry and attended to her cheeks with the powder rag. She stood by the window and looked out dully at a grey cat walking a grey fence in a grey backyard. To-morrow would be Christmas Day, and she had only $1.87 with which to buy Jim a present. She had been saving every penny she could for months, with this result. Twenty dollars a week doesn't go far. Expenses had been greater than she had calculated. They always are. Only $1.87 to buy a present for Jim. Her Jim. Many a happy hour she had spent planning for something nice for him. Something fine and rare and sterling—something just a little bit near to being worthy of the honour of being owned by Jim.

There was a pier-glass between the windows of the room. Perhaps you have seen a pier-glass in an $8 flat. A very thin and very agile person may, by observing his reflection in a rapid sequence of longitudinal strips, obtain a fairly accurate conception of his looks. Della, being slender, had mastered the art.

Suddenly she whirled from the window and stood before the glass. Her eyes were shining brilliantly, but her face had lost its colour within twenty seconds. Rapidly she pulled down her hair and let it fall to its full length.

Now, there were two possessions of the James Dillingham Youngs in which they both took a mighty pride. One was Jim's gold watch that had been his father's and his grandfather's. The other was Della's hair. Had the Queen of Sheba lived in the flat across the airshaft, Della would have let her hair hang out the window some day to dry just to depreciate Her Majesty's jewels and gifts. Had King Solomon been the janitor, with all his treasures piled up in the basement, Jim would have pulled out his watch every time he passed, just to see him pluck at his beard from envy.

So now Della's beautiful hair fell about her, rippling and shining like a cascade of brown waters. It reached below her knee and made itself almost a garment for her. And then she did it up again nervously and quickly. Once she faltered for a minute and stood still while a tear or two splashed on the worn red carpet.

On went her old brown jacket; on went her old brown hat. With a whirl of skirts and with the brilliant sparkle still in her eyes, she fluttered out the door and down the stairs to the street.

Where she stopped the sign read: "Mme. Sofronie. Hair Goods of All Kinds." One flight up Della ran, and collected herself, panting. Madame, large, too white, chilly, hardly looked the "Sofronie."

"Will you buy my hair?" asked Della.

"I buy hair," said Madame. "Take yer hat off and let's have a sight at the looks of it."

Down rippled the brown cascade.

"Twenty dollars," said Madame, lifting the mass with a practised hand.

"Give it to me quick," said Della.

Oh, and the next two hours tripped by on rosy wings. Forget the hashed metaphor. She was ransacking the stores for Jim's present.

She found it at last. It surely had been made for Jim and no one else. There was no other like it in any of the stores, and she had turned all of them inside out. It was a platinum fob chain simple and chaste in design, properly proclaiming its value by substance alone and not by meretricious ornamentation—as all good things should do. It was even worthy of The Watch. As soon as she saw it she knew that it must be Jim's. It was like him. Quietness and value—the description applied to both. Twenty-one dollars they took from her for it, and she hurried home with the 87 cents. With that chain on his watch Jim might be properly anxious about the time in any company. Grand as the watch was, he sometimes looked at it on the sly on account of the old leather strap that he used in place of a chain.

When Della reached home her intoxication gave way a little to prudence and reason. She got out her curling irons and lighted the gas and went to work repairing the ravages made by generosity added to love. Which is always a tremendous task, dear friends—a mammoth task.

Within forty minutes her head was covered with tiny, close-lying curls that made her look wonderfully like a truant school-boy. She looked at her reflection in the mirror long, carefully, and critically.

"If Jim doesn't kill me," she said to herself, "before he takes a second look at me, he'll say I look like a Coney Island chorus girl. But what could I do—oh! what could I do with a dollar and eighty-seven cents?"

At 7 o'clock the coffee was made and the frying-pan was on the back of the stove hot and ready to cook the chops.

Jim was never late. Della doubled the fob chain in her hand and sat on the corner of the table near the door that he always entered. Then she heard his step on the stair away down on the first flight, and she turned white for just a moment. She had a habit of saying little silent prayers about the simplest everyday things, and now she whispered: "Please God, make him think I am still pretty."

The door opened and Jim stepped in and closed it. He looked thin and very serious. Poor fellow, he was only twenty-two—and to be burdened with a family! He needed a new overcoat and he was without gloves.

Jim stopped inside the door, as immovable as a setter at the scent of quail. His eyes were fixed upon Della, and there was an expression in them that she could not read, and it terrified her. It was not anger, nor surprise, nor disapproval, nor horror, nor any of the sentiments that she had been prepared for. He simply stared at her fixedly with that peculiar expression on his face.

Della wriggled off the table and went for him.

"Jim, darling," she cried, "don't look at me that way. I had my hair cut off and sold it because I couldn't have lived through Christmas without giving you a present. It'll grow out again—you won't mind, will you? I just had to do it. My hair grows awfully fast. Say 'Merry Christmas!' Jim, and let's be happy. You don't know what a nice—what a beautiful, nice gift I've got for you."

"You've cut off your hair?" asked Jim, laboriously, as if he had not arrived at that patent fact yet even after the hardest mental labour.

"Cut it off and sold it," said Della. "Don't you like me just as well, anyhow? I'm me without my hair, ain't I?"

Jim looked about the room curiously.

"You say your hair is gone?" he said, with an air almost of idiocy.

"You needn't look for it," said Della. "It's sold, I tell you—sold and gone, too. It's Christmas Eve, boy. Be good to me, for it went for you. Maybe the hairs of my head were numbered," she went on with a sudden serious sweetness, "but nobody could ever count my love for you. Shall I put the chops on, Jim?"

Out of his trance Jim seemed quickly to wake. He enfolded his Della. For ten seconds let us regard with discreet scrutiny some inconsequential object in the other direction. Eight dollars a week or a million a year—what is the difference? A mathematician or a wit would give you the wrong answer. The magi brought valuable gifts, but that was not among them. This dark assertion will be illuminated later on.

Jim drew a package from his overcoat pocket and threw it upon the table.

"Don't make any mistake, Dell," he said, "about me. I don't think there's anything in the way of a haircut or a shave or a shampoo that could make me like my girl any less. But if you'll unwrap that package you may see why you had me going a while at first."

White fingers and nimble tore at the string and paper. And then an ecstatic scream of joy; and then, alas! a quick feminine change to hysterical tears and wails, necessitating the immediate employment of all the comforting powers of the lord of the flat.

For there lay The Combs—the set of combs, side and back, that Della had worshipped for long in a Broadway window. Beautiful combs, pure tortoise shell, with jewelled rims—just the shade to wear in the beautiful vanished hair. They were expensive combs, she knew, and her heart had simply craved and yearned over them without the least hope of possession. And now, they were hers, but the tresses that should have adorned the coveted adornments were gone.

But she hugged them to her bosom, and at length she was able to look up with dim eyes and a smile and say: "My hair grows so fast, Jim!"

And then Della leaped up like a little singed cat and cried, "Oh, oh!"

Jim had not yet seen his beautiful present. She held it out to him eagerly upon her open palm. The dull precious metal seemed to flash with a reflection of her bright and ardent spirit.

"Isn't it a dandy, Jim? I hunted all over town to find it. You'll have to look at the time a hundred times a day now. Give me your watch. I want to see how it looks on it."

Instead of obeying, Jim tumbled down on the couch and put his hands under the back of his head and smiled.

"Dell," said he, "let's put our Christmas presents away and keep 'em a while. They're too nice to use just at present. I sold the watch to get the money to buy your combs. And now suppose you put the chops on."

The magi, as you know, were wise men—wonderfully wise men—who brought gifts to the Babe in the manger. They invented the art of giving Christmas presents. Being wise, their gifts were no doubt wise ones, possibly bearing the privilege of exchange in case of duplication. And here I have lamely related to you the uneventful chronicle of two foolish children in a flat who most unwisely sacrificed for each other the greatest treasures of their house. But in a last word to the wise of these days let it be said that of all who give gifts these two were the wisest. Of all who give and receive gifts, such as they are wisest. Everywhere they are wisest. They are the magi.

COMPLIMENTS OF THE SEASON

THERE are no more Christmas stories to write. Fiction is exhausted; and newspaper items, the next best, are manufactured by clever young journalists who have married early and have an engagingly pessimistic view of life. Therefore, for seasonable diversion, we are reduced to two very questionable sources—facts and philosophy. We will begin with—whichever you choose to call it.

Children are pestilential little animals with which we have to cope under a bewildering variety of conditions. Especially when childish sorrows overwhelm them are we put to our wits' end. We exhaust our paltry store of consolation; and then beat them, sobbing, to sleep. Then we grovel in the dust of a million years, and ask God why. Thus we call out of the rattrap. As for the children, no one understands them except old maids, hunchbacks, and shepherd dogs.

Now come the facts in the case of the Rag-Doll, the Tatterdemalion, and the Twenty-fifth of December.

On the tenth of that month the Child of the Millionaire lost her rag-doll. There were many servants in the Millionaire's palace on the Hudson, and these ransacked the house and grounds, but without finding the lost treasure. The child was a girl of five, and one of those perverse little beasts that often wound the sensibilities of wealthy parents by fixing their affections upon some vulgar, inexpensive toy instead of upon diamond-studded automobiles and pony phaetons.

The Child grieved sorely and truly, a thing inexplicable to the Millionaire, to whom the rag-doll market was about as interesting as Bay State Gas; and to the Lady, the Child's mother, who was all for form—that is, nearly all, as you shall see.

The Child cried inconsolably, and grew hollow-eyed, knock-kneed, spindling, and corykilverty in many other respects. The Millionaire smiled and tapped his coffers confidently. The pick of the output of the French and German toymakers was rushed by special delivery to the mansion; but Rachel refused to be comforted. She was weeping for her rag child, and was for a high protective tariff against all foreign foolishness. Then doctors with the finest bedside manners and stop-watches were called in. One by one they chattered futilely about peptomanganate of iron and sea voyages and hypophosphites until their stop-watches showed that Bill Rendered was under the wire for show or place. Then, as men, they advised that the rag-doll be found as soon as possible and restored to its mourning parent. The Child sniffed at therapeutics, chewed a thumb, and wailed for her Betsy. And all this time cablegrams were coming from Santa Claus saying that he would soon be here and enjoining us to show a true Christian spirit and let up on the poolrooms and tontine policies and platoon systems long enough to give him a welcome. Everywhere the spirit of Christmas was diffusing itself. The banks were refusing loans, the pawn-brokers had doubled their gang of helpers, people bumped your shins on the streets with red sleds, Thomas and Jeremiah bubbled before you on the bars while you waited on one foot, holly-wreaths of hospitality were hung in windows of the stores, they who had 'em were getting out their furs. You hardly knew which was the best bet in balls—three, high, moth, or snow. It was no time at which to lose the rag-doll of your heart.

If Doctor Watson's investigating friend had been called in to solve this mysterious disappearance he might have observed on the Millionaire's wall a copy of "The Vampire." That would have quickly suggested, by induction, "A rag and a bone and a hank of hair." "Flip," a Scotch terrier, next to the rag-doll in the Child's heart, frisked through the halls. The hank of hair! Aha! X, the unfound quantity, represented the rag-doll. But, the bone? Well, when dogs find bones they——Done! It were an easy and a fruitful task to examine Flip's forefeet. Look, Watson! Earth—dried earth between the toes. Of course, the dog—but Sherlock was not there. Therefore it devolves. But topography and architecture must intervene.

The Millionaire's palace occupied a lordly space. In front of it was a lawn close-mowed as a South Ireland man's face two days after a shave. At one side of it, and fronting on another street was a pleasaunce trimmed to a leaf, and the garage and stables. The Scotch pup had ravished the rag-doll from the nursery, dragged it to a corner of the lawn, dug a hole, and buried it after the manner of careless undertakers. There you have the mystery solved, and no checks to write for the hypodermical wizard or fi'-pun notes to toss to the sergeant. Then let's get down to the heart of the thing, tiresome readers—the Christmas heart of the thing.

Fuzzy was drunk—not riotously or helplessly or loquaciously, as you or I might get, but decently, appropriately, and inoffensively, as becomes a gentleman down on his luck.

Fuzzy was a soldier of misfortune. The road, the haystack, the park bench, the kitchen door, the bitter round of eleemosynary beds-with-shower-bath-attachment, the petty pickings and ignobly garnered largesse of great cities—these formed the chapters of his history.

Fuzzy walked toward the river, down the street that bounded one side of the Millionaire's house and grounds. He saw a leg of Betsy, the lost rag-doll, protruding, like the clue to a Lilliputian murder mystery, from its untimely grave in a corner of the fence. He dragged forth the maltreated infant, tucked it under his arm, and went on his way crooning a road song of his brethren that no doll that has been brought up to the sheltered life should hear. Well for Betsy that she had no ears. And well that she had no eyes save unseeing circles of black; for the faces of Fuzzy and the Scotch terrier were those of brothers, and the heart of no rag-doll could withstand twice to become the prey of such fearsome monsters.

Though you may not know it, Grogan's saloon stands near the river and near the foot of the street down which Fuzzy traveled. In Grogan's, Christmas cheer was already rampant.

Fuzzy entered with his doll. He fancied that as a mummer at the feast of Saturn he might earn a few drops from the wassail cup.

He set Betsy on the bar and addressed her loudly and humorously, seasoning his speech with exaggerated compliments and endearments, as one entertaining his lady friend. The loafers and bibbers around caught the farce of it, and roared. The bartender gave Fuzzy a drink. Oh, many of us carry rag-dolls.

"One for the lady?" suggested Fuzzy impudently, and tucked another contribution to Art beneath his waistcoat.

He began to see possibilities in Betsy. His first-night had been a success. Visions of a vaudeville circuit about town dawned upon him.

In a group near the stove sat "Pigeon" McCarthy,

Black Riley, and "One-ear" Mike, well and unfavorably known in the tough shoestring district that blackened the left bank of the river. They passed a newspaper back and forth among themselves. The item that each solid and blunt forefinger pointed out was an advertisement headed "One Hundred Dollars Reward." To earn it one must return the rag-doll lost, strayed, or stolen from the Millionaire's mansion. It seemed that grief still ravaged, unchecked, in the bosom of the too faithful Child. Flip, the terrier, capered and shook his absurd whisker before her, powerless to distract. She wailed for her Betsy in the faces of walking, talking, mamaing, and eye-closing French Mabelles and Violettes. The advertisement was a last resort.

Black Riley came from behind the stove and approached Fuzzy in his one-sided parabolic way.

The Christmas mummer, flushed with success, had tucked Betsy under his arm, and was about to depart to the filling of impromptu dates elsewhere.

"Say, 'Bo," said Black Riley to him, "where did you cop out dat doll?"

"This doll?" asked Fuzzy, touching Betsy with his forefinger to be sure that she was the one referred to. "Why, this doll was presented to me by the Emperor of Beloochistan. I have seven hundred others in my country home in Newport. This doll——"

"Cheese the funny business," said Riley. "You swiped it or picked it up at de house on de hill where

—but never mind dat. You want to take fifty cents for de rags, and take it quick. Me brother's kid at home might be wantin' to play wid it. Hey—what?"

He produced the coin.

Fuzzy laughed a gurgling, insolent, alcoholic laugh in his face. Go to the office of Sarah Bernhardt's manager and propose to him that she be released from a night's performance to entertain the Tackytown Lyceum and Literary Coterie. You will hear the duplicate of Fuzzy's laugh.

Black Riley gauged Fuzzy quickly with his blueberry eye as a wrestler does. His hand was itching to play the Roman and wrest the rag Sabine from the extemporaneous merry-andrew who was entertaining an angel unaware. But he refrained. Fuzzy was fat and solid and big. Three inches of well-nourished corporeity, defended from the winter winds by dingy linen, intervened between his vest and trousers. Countless small, circular wrinkles running around his coat-sleeves and knees guaranteed the quality of his bone and muscle. His small, blue eyes, bathed in the moisture of altruism and wooziness, looked upon you kindly, yet without abashment. He was whiskerly, whiskyly, fleshily formidable. So, Black Riley temporized.

"Wot'll you take for it, den?" he asked.

"Money," said Fuzzy, with husky firmness, "cannot buy her."

He was intoxicated with the artist's first sweet cup of attainment. To set a faded-blue, earth-stained rag-doll on a bar, to hold mimic converse with it, and to find his heart leaping with the sense of plaudits earned and his throat scorching with free libations poured in his honor—could base coin buy him from such achievements? You will perceive that Fuzzy had the temperament.

Fuzzy walked out with the gait of a trained sea-lion in search of other cafés to conquer.

Though the dusk of twilight was hardly yet apparent, lights were beginning to spangle the city like pop-corn bursting in a deep skillet. Christmas Eve, impatiently expected, was peeping over the brink of the hour. Millions had prepared for its celebration. Towns would be painted red. You, yourself, have heard the horns and dodged the capers of the Saturnalians.

"Pigeon" McCarthy, Black Riley, and "One-ear" Mike held a hasty converse outside Grogan's. They were narrow-chested, pallid striplings, not fighters in the open, but more dangerous in their ways of warfare than the most terrible of Turks. Fuzzy, in a pitched battle, could have eaten the three of them. In a go-as-you-please encounter he was already doomed.

They overtook him just as he and Betsy were entering Costigan's Casino. They deflected him, and shoved the newspaper under his nose. Fuzzy could read—and more.

"Boys," said he, "you are certainly damn true friends. Give me a week to think it over."

The soul of a real artist is quenched with difficulty.

The boys carefully pointed out to him that advertisements were soulless, and that the deficiencies of the day might not be supplied by the morrow.

"A cool hundred," said Fuzzy thoughtfully and mushily.

"Boys," said he, "you are true friends. I'll go up and claim the reward. The show business is not what it used to be."

Night was falling more surely. The three tagged at his sides to the foot of the rise on which stood the Millionaire's house. There Fuzzy turned upon them acrimoniously.

"You are a pack of putty-faced beagle-hounds," he roared. "Go away."

They went away—a little way.

In "Pigeon" McCarthy's pocket was a section of one-inch gas-pipe eight inches long. In one end of it and in the middle of it was a lead plug. One-half of it was packed tight with solder. Black Riley carried a slung-shot, being a conventional thug. "One-ear" Mike relied upon a pair of brass knucks—an heirloom in the family.

"Why fetch and carry," said Black Riley, "when some one will do it for ye? Let him bring it out to us. Hey—what?"

"We can chuck him in the river," said "Pigeon" McCarthy, "with a stone tied to his feet."

"Youse guys make me tired," said "One-ear"

Mike sadly. "Ain't progress ever appealed to none of yez? Sprinkle a little gasoline on 'im, and drop 'im on the Drive—well?"

Fuzzy entered the Millionaire's gate and zigzagged toward the softly glowing entrance of the mansion. The three goblins came up to the gate and lingered—one on each side of it, one beyond the roadway. They fingered their cold metal and leather, confident.

Fuzzy rang the door-bell, smiling foolishly and dreamily. An atavistic instinct prompted him to reach for the button of his right glove. But he wore no gloves; so his left hand dropped, embarrassed.

The particular menial whose duty it was to open doors to silks and laces shied at first sight of Fuzzy. But a second glance took in his passport, his card of admission, his surety of welcome—the lost ragdoll of the daughter of the house dangling under his arm.

Fuzzy was admitted into a great hall, dim with the glow from unseen lights. The hireling went away and returned with a maid and the Child. The doll was restored to the mourning one. She clasped her lost darling to her breast; and then, with the inordinate selfishness and candor of childhood, stamped her foot and whined hatred and fear of the odious being who had rescued her from the depths of sorrow and despair. Fuzzy wriggled himself into an ingratiatory attitude and essayed the idiotic smile and blattering small talk that is supposed to charm the budding intellect of the young. The Child bawled, and was dragged away, hugging her Betsy close.

There came the Secretary, pale, poised, polished, gliding in pumps, and worshipping pomp and ceremony. He counted out into Fuzzy's hand ten ten-dollar bills; then dropped his eye upon the door, transferred it to James, its custodian, indicated the obnoxious earner of the reward with the other, and allowed his pumps to waft him away to secretarial regions.

James gathered Fuzzy with his own commanding optic and swept him as far as the front door.

When the money touched Fuzzy's dingy palm his first instinct was to take to his heels; but a second thought restrained him from that blunder of etiquette. It was his; it had been given him. It—and, oh, what an elysium it opened to the gaze of his mind's eye! He had tumbled to the foot of the ladder; he was hungry, homeless, friendless, ragged, cold, drifting; and he held in his hand the key to a paradise of the mud-honey that he craved. The fairy doll had waved a wand with her rag-stuffed hand; and now wherever he might go the enchanted palaces with shining foot-rests and magic red fluids in gleaming glassware would be open to him.

He followed James to the door.

He paused there as the flunky drew open the great mahogany portal for him to pass into the vestibule.

Beyond the wrought-iron gates in the dark highway Black Riley and his two pals casually strolled, fingering under their coats the inevitably fatal weapons that were to make the reward of the rag-doll theirs.

Fuzzy stopped at the Millionaire's door and bethought himself. Like little sprigs of mistletoe on a dead tree, certain living green thoughts and memories began to decorate his confused mind. He was quite drunk, mind you, and the present was beginning to fade. Those wreaths and festoons of holly with their scarlet berries making the great hall gay—where had he seen such things before? Somewhere he had known polished floors and odors of fresh flowers in winter, and—and some one was singing a song in the house that he thought he had heard before. Some one singing and playing a harp. Of course, it was Christmas—Fuzzy thought he must have been pretty drunk to have overlooked that.

And then he went out of the present, and there came back to him out of some impossible, vanished, and irrevocable past a little, pure-white, transient, forgotten ghost—the spirit of *noblesse oblige*. Upon a gentleman certain things devolve.

James opened the outer door. A stream of light went down the graveled walk to the iron gate. Black Riley, McCarthy, and "One-ear" Mike saw, and carelessly drew their sinister cordon closer about the gate.

With a more imperious gesture than James's master had ever used or could ever use, Fuzzy compelled the menial to close the door. Upon a gentleman certain things devolve. Especially at the Christmas season.

"It is cust—custormary," he said to James, the flustered, "when a gentleman calls on Christmas Eve to pass the compliments of the season with the lady of the house. You und'stand? I shall not move shtep till I pass compl'ments season with lady the house. Und'stand?"

There was an argument. James lost. Fuzzy raised his voice and sent it through the house unpleasantly. I did not say he was a gentleman. He was simply a tramp being visited by a ghost.

A sterling silver bell rang. James went back to answer it, leaving Fuzzy in the hall. James explained somewhere to some one.

Then he came and conducted Fuzzy into the library.

The lady entered a moment later. She was more beautiful and holy than any picture that Fuzzy had seen. She smiled, and said something about a doll. Fuzzy didn't understand that; he remembered nothing about a doll.

A footman brought in two small glasses of sparkling wine on a stamped sterling-silver waiter. The Lady took one. The other was handed to Fuzzy.

As his fingers closed on the slender glass stem his disabilities dropped from him for one brief moment. He straightened himself; and Time, so disobliging to most of us, turned backward to accommodate Fuzzy.

Forgotten Christmas ghosts whiter than the false beards of the most opulent Kriss Kringle were rising in the fumes of Grogan's whisky. What had the Millionaire's mansion to do with a long, wainscoted Virginia hall, where the riders were grouped around a silver punch-bowl, drinking the ancient toast of the House? And why should the patter of the cab horses' hoofs on the frozen street be in any wise related to the sound of the saddled hunters stamping under the shelter of the west veranda? And what had Fuzzy to do with any of it?

The Lady, looking at him over her glass, let her condescending smile fade away like a false dawn. Her eyes turned serious. She saw something beneath the rags and Scotch terrier whiskers that she did not understand. But it did not matter.

Fuzzy lifted his glass and smiled vacantly.

"P-pardon, lady," he said, "but couldn't leave without exchangin' comp'ments sheason with lady th' house. 'Gainst princ'ples gen'leman do sho."

And then he began the ancient salutation that was a tradition in the House when men wore lace ruffles and powder.

"The blessings of another year——"

Fuzzy's memory failed him. The Lady prompted:

"——Be upon this hearth."

"——The guest——" stammered Fuzzy.

"——And upon her who——" continued the Lady, with a leading smile.

"Oh, cut it out," said Fuzzy, ill-manneredly. "I can't remember. Drink hearty."

Fuzzy had shot his arrow. They drank. The Lady smiled again the smile of her caste. James enveloped Fuzzy and re-conducted him toward the front door. The harp music still softly drifted through the house.

Outside, Black Riley breathed on his cold hands and hugged the gate.

"I wonder," said the Lady to herself, musing, "who—but there were so many who came. I wonder whether memory is a curse or a blessing to them after they have fallen so low."

Fuzzy and his escort were nearly at the door. The Lady called: "James!"

James stalked back obsequiously, leaving Fuzzy waiting unsteadily, with his brief spark of the divine fire gone.

Outside, Black Riley stamped his cold feet and got a firmer grip on his section of gas-pipe.

"You will conduct this gentleman," said the Lady, "downstairs. Then tell Louis to get out the Mercedes and take him to whatever place he wishes to go."

ABOUT THE AUTHOR

The following biography is adapted from the more exten-sive Chronology in O. Henry: 101 Stories, *edited by Ben Yagoda (Library of America, 2021).*

WILLIAM SIDNEY PORTER was born on September 11, 1862, in Greensboro, North Carolina, the second of three sons of Algernon Sidney Porter and Mary Jane Virginia Swaim. Shortly after William's third birthday, his mother died of tuberculosis, and his younger brother, who had been born in March, died later that year. At the age of five, William was enrolled in a small private school operated by a maternal aunt and remained a student there for nine years.

In 1877, his formal schooling at an end, William, known as "Will" to his friends, began to work in the drugstore of his father's brother, and four years later became a registered pharmacist with the North Carolina Pharmaceutical Association. When he was nineteen, he developed a persistent cough, and a local doctor, James K. Hall, invited Porter to travel with him to Texas, where the Halls' four sons lived. He spent two years performing undemanding tasks at the sheep ranch of one of the sons, Richard, in La

Salle County. In March 1884, he moved to Austin, found work as a drug clerk in a pharmacy, quit after three months, and became a member of the Hill City Quartet, which performed at various venues around town. He subsequently became a bookkeeper for a real estate firm and then, for four years, a draftsman in the Texas Land Office.

During this period, he met Athol Estes, an Austin high school girl originally from Tennessee and, just weeks after her graduation in 1887, the couple were married—without informing Athol's mother or step-father beforehand. On September 30, 1889, Athol gave birth to their daughter, Margaret, but began to show signs of the tuberculosis that had killed her father and that would plague her for the rest of her life.

Embezzlement Trial and Conviction

In 1891, after the election of a new governor, Porter lost his job in the Land Office because his political patron was forced out of his own position, and he became a teller at the First National Bank. In December 1894, discrepancies were found in Porter's books at the bank, and he resigned. At a U.S. grand jury hearing the following July, bank examiner F. B. Gray presented evidence that on fifty occasions Porter embezzled bank funds, for a total of $5,654.20; bank employees testified, to the contrary, that the discrepancies were a result of an unfortunate series of errors.

He was not indicted at that hearing but, in February, Gray resubmitted a narrower set of accusations to the grand jury, which voted to indict. Arrested in Houston, Porter was taken to Austin and released on bond after two days in jail. In July 1896, instead of showing up for his trial, he fled without his family to New Orleans and, several weeks later, traveled by boat to Honduras, the only Central American country that had no extradition laws with the United States.

The following January, because of Athol's poor health, Porter returned to Austin, again traveling through New Orleans, and turned himself in. During the next several months he nursed his wife, who died on July 25 at the age of twenty-nine.

Porter's trial took place in February 1898. He asked his family and friends to stay away from the courtroom. (One of his defense attorneys later said, "How could I defend him? How could anybody have defended him when he wouldn't defend himself? He wouldn't talk.") Gray focused on two of the missing deposits, totaling about $850, and during the three-day trial, witnesses, backed up by documents, testified that the deposits were made at the First National Bank, that Porter received the cash, and that he did not record the transactions. Deliberating for less than a day, the jury reached a guilty verdict. In March 1898, Porter was sentenced to five years in the Ohio State Penitentiary, the minimum sentence allowed, and he entered the prison on April 25. His daughter, Margaret, was given over to the care of Athol's mother and stepfather, who told their granddaughter that Porter was employed as a traveling salesman. Porter was released after three years and three months, on July 24, 1901, his sentence having been reduced for good behavior.

LITERARY CAREER AND LATER LIFE

Porter began writing for publication after he first moved to Austin; in 1887, he sent humorous verse, sketches, and jokes to the Detroit *Free Press* and to the New York weekly *Truth*. In 1894, he founded, edited, and wrote much of the material for a Texas-based, eight-page weekly humor paper, *The Rolling Stone*, which he produced in his spare time from his work at the bank. Never reaching a circulation higher than 1,500, it suspended publication the following year. While his activities at the bank were under investigation by authorities, he accepted a job at *The Houston Post*, moved to Houston, and contributed cartoons and a daily column, "Some Postscripts," under the pen name "The Post Man."

Before his trial began, Porter sold his first proper short story, "The Miracle of Lava Canyon," a Western tale, to the McClure Syndicate, which published it under the byline W. S. Porter. It was about this time that Porter began spelling his middle name Sydney. While he was in prison, he submitted numerous stories for publication, and three of them appeared in print under the name "O. Henry."

After Porter's release from prison, he traveled to Pittsburgh to be reunited with his mother-in-law and twelve-year-old Margaret, who had moved there when Athol's stepfather found work managing a hotel. Porter stayed in the hotel for about nine months, during which nine stories and several poems were published under various pseudonyms in national magazines, including some of the tales he wrote in prison. Gilman Hall, the editor of *Ainslee's*, which had already accepted several of his stories, advanced $200 so that Porter could move to New York. He arrived in April 1902, while Margaret remained in Pittsburgh with her grandparents. During the remaining eight years of his life, nearly all of which were spent in Manhattan, he wrote more than two hundred stories and concealed his time in prison from his friends and associates.

In December 1903, O. Henry (as he now signed all his pieces) contracted with the *New York Sunday World* magazine to contribute a selection every week; over the next two years he wrote 113 stories, including such classics as "The Furnished Room," "The Last Leaf," and "The Gift of the Magi." In 1904, McClure, Phillips & Co. published his first book, *Cabbages and Kings*, interconnected stories set in a fictional Central American country. Two years later he published his second and most successful book, *The Four Million*, a collection of stories set in New York and almost entirely reprinted from his contributions to the *World*. During the last three years of his life, an additional six collections appeared, and three more books were published in the months after his death.

O. Henry's ability to make respectable amounts of money writing short stories was far surpassed by both his profligacy and generosity. He received hefty advances from numerous magazines for far more stories than he could produce—as well as $1,500 for a novel he never began—and often had to return advances he had already spent. Desperate for cash, he sold the rights for "A Retrieved Reformation" to the-atrical producer George Tyler for a flat fee of $500. In a matter of weeks, the story was adapted for the stage by Paul Armstrong and opened in Chicago as *Alias Jimmy Valentine*, a melodrama that became an inter-national success, earning the playwright more than $100,000 in a year and even more for the producer.

In November 1907, O. Henry married Sara Cole-man, a childhood sweetheart still living in North Carolina; the marriage was unhappy from the start. Afflicted with poor health from years of heavy drink-ing, he was increasingly stressed by the need to sup-port the two of them and Margaret (who now lived with the couple). They moved to Asheville during the fall and winter of 1909–10 but he returned to New York, ostensibly to work on a new play for the stage. Instead, he remained lethargic and mostly shut up in his room, his health declining.

On June 3, 1910, O. Henry telephoned Anne Part-lan, one of his earliest friends in New York, and con-veyed an urgent request for help. She arrived at his apartment to find him semiconscious; a doctor had him admitted to Polyclinic Hospital on East 34th Street. Diagnosed with cirrhosis of the liver, diabetes, and a dilated heart, he died on the morning of June 5, some three months before his forty-eighth birthday.

ABOUT THE STORIES

THE PURPLE DRESS

First published in *The New York Sunday World*
(November 5, 1905)
Collected in *The Trimmed Lamp* (1907)

BEFORE William Sydney Porter became the famous author O. Henry, he read various magazine sketches by a writer named Anne Partlan, who scraped out a living by designing advertisements, selling humorous anecdotes to publications, and taking on assorted menial work. After he arrived in New York City, Porter looked Partlan up and she showed him around town and introduced him to her friends. "He had absolutely no pose," she recalled. "That is why there is never anything sordid in [his] little stories. We were poor enough in our dingy rooms, but he saw the little pleasures and surprises that made life bearable to us."

What distinguished his writings about working women from the usual sentimental pap was their lack of moralizing, at least in his depictions of the employees. (Managers and business owners, however, did not always escape his judgment.) The stories barely touched on the women's work in shops and offices but instead focused on their lives and poverty, their hopes and disappointments—or, as in "The Purple Dress," their anticipation and enjoyment of a social event, like a Thanksgiving dinner party. One friend recalled when he asked O. Henry about his shopgirl stories, "Do you ever go into the department stores to study them?" "Indeed, not," he answered. "It is not the sales-girl *in* the department store who is worth studying, it is the sales-girl *out* of it."

Other than castigating employers for not paying a livable wage to working-class women, O. Henry did not advocate specific policies or actions. Yet his stories had their effect; he incorporated in their plots the simple arithmetic showing the impossibility of surviving on five dollars a week in the city he called "Bagdad-on-the-Subway." Magazines and newspapers at the time pointed to his stories when discussing the plight of young single women. One editorialist wrote, "Across every counter of the New York department store is the shadow of O. Henry." Former president Theodore Roosevelt became involved in a citywide campaign during 1912–13 to improve the wages of female store and office workers; "It was O. Henry who started me on my campaign for office girls!" he later wrote in a letter to C. Alphonso Smith, O. Henry's first biographer.

His reputation as a friend and advocate of underpaid women endured for several decades. Five years after O. Henry died, the author Christopher Morley published in *The Saturday Evening Post* a sonnet that included the lines:

But still the heart of his well-loved Bagdad
Upon-the-Subway is to him renewed.
He knew, beneath her harmless platitude,
The gentler secrets that the shopgirl had.

In the story:

"Oh, pshaw!" it wasn't G. Bernard they meant at all. O. Henry puns on the name of the Irish playwright G. Bernard Shaw, who also became an advocate for better wages and conditions for women workers. His play *Mrs. Warren's Profession* had been published in 1898 and first performed in 1902; Shaw's preface explains that it was written "to draw attention to the truth that prostitution is caused . . . by underpaying, undervaluing and overworking women so shamefully that the poorest of them are forced to resort to prostitution to keep body and soul together." The American premiere took place at the Garrick Theatre in New York on October 30, 1905—only one week before O. Henry published his story. The opening night performance was sold out, with nearly 1,000 in the audience—including Police Commissioner William McAdoo and several members of the city's vice squad. The next day, arrest warrants were issued for most of the cast and crew, including the star, Mary Shaw (no relation), the producer, Arnold Daly, and the theater manager, Samuel W. Gumpertz. The hearing was postponed and the cast released, but the production was shut down for violating the city's Comstock law. At the trial the following July, all involved were acquitted. Mary Shaw would reprise her role with a modified cast for a March 1907 production that ran for twenty-five performances.

Pull-bone was a common word for wishbone, in this case probably from a turkey.

Two Thanksgiving Day Gentlemen

First published in *The New York Sunday World*
(November 26, 1905)
Collected in *The Trimmed Lamp* (1907)

Throughout his decade in New York, O. Henry was constantly in debt. He owed money to friends and in-laws from his Texas days; he had borrowed heavily against advances for stories not yet written or conceived. He would fulfill some debts, with either stories or cash, only to borrow some more. After he died, those who knew him, even those to whom he owed money, would dismiss those obligations and instead regale reporters and biographers with stories about the extraordinary amounts he gave away to the neediest cases he met on the street. One bartender told a *New York Times* reporter, "If he had $10 he'd give it to you, and then perhaps come over and borrow a half dollar from me. He was always helping some of the boys out, and never a come-back. I've heard that from lots of people." Some of the anecdotes might have been apocryphal or embellished; there's a famous tale about the tramp who chased O. Henry down the street because he thought the author had mistakenly given him a twenty-dollar bill (or gold piece, in some versions) instead of a dollar. O. Henry is supposed to have said, "I know it is, but it's all I have." Or maybe, embarrassed his generosity was exposed in front of a companion, he replied testily, "Don't you think I know what a dollar is? Move along." The contradictions and variations in no way undercut the abundance of recollections indicating that, while O. Henry may have made thousands of dollars on his writing, he gave much of it to the down-and-out denizens of the city who populated his stories.

O. Henry's desire to provide companionship and comfort to the destitute dates to his days in Austin. Two years after his death, Dixie Daniels, one of the partners on *The Rolling Stone*, recalled in a *Dallas Morning News* article:

> He was one of the genuine democrats that you hear about more often than you meet. Night after night, after we would shut up shop, he would call to me to come along and "go bumming." That was his favorite expression for the night-time prowling in which we indulged. We would wander through streets and alleys, meeting with some of the worst specimens of down-and-outers it has ever been my privilege to see at close range. I've seen the most ragged specimen of a bum hold up Porter, who would always do anything he could for the man. His one great failing was his inability to say "No" to a man.

Three of the stories in this collection have homeless men as their protagonists. "Two Thanksgiving Day Gentlemen" differs from the others because the gift of a luxurious Thanksgiving dinner is not a reward for some heroic or generous act on the part of the tramp. Instead, Stuffy Pete's annual meal is given without the expectation of reciprocity by a "gentleman" who can hardly afford it—and who might as well be a stand-in for O. Henry himself.

In the story:

Each year, the American president issues a proclamation officially confirming the date for Thanksgiving; on November 2, 1905, three weeks before the story was published, Theodore **Roosevelt** issued his annual message that "set apart Thursday, the 30th day of this November, as a day of thanksgiving for the past and of prayer for the future." **Saleratus biscuits** are made from baking soda. **Kind Salvation fingers** refers to the volunteers of the Salvation Army. Alberto **Santos-Dumont** was a Brazilian inventor who, at the beginning of the twentieth century, made several of the first powered manned flights in Europe, including the first recorded on film. A **crown of imperishable bay** symbolizes eternal reward, as mentioned in 1 Corinthians 9:25 ("Now they do it to obtain a corruptible crown; but we an incorruptible"); bay is another word for the evergreen laurel shrub used in ancient Greece to crown the victors in the Pythian games.

WHISTLING DICK'S CHRISTMAS STOCKING
First published in *McClure's Magazine* (December 1899)
Collected in *Roads of Destiny* (1909)

"Whistling Dick's Christmas Stocking" was not only the first story by William Sydney Porter published in a national magazine; it was also the first to appear under his pseudonym "O. Henry." That the editors of *McClure's Magazine* agreed to publish it at all is thanks largely to a fortuitous absence when they were preparing the Christmas issue of 1899.

McClure's fiction editor Viola Roseboro' (who discarded her unapostrophed family name, Roseborough, after an earlier acting career) began sending encouraging letters to Porter in response to stories he had submitted—even though his stories were not quite appropriate for the magazine. The McClure newspaper syndicate had published Porter's first short story, "The Miracle of Lava Canyon," but when it came to fiction in his magazine, S. S. McClure's ambition was to present for a mass audience literary works of a higher class; he favored established authors of genteel prose and compared *McClure's* to a gentleman entering a family home. In the fall of 1899, however, McClure was away in Europe and his partner, John Sanborn Phillips, was ill. Roseboro' and Ida Tarbell, who had just recently been made a full-time desk editor, were left in charge of putting together the Christmas issue. Faced with a dearth of acceptable holiday stories, Roseboro' thought Porter's story "publishable" and "felt anxious to encourage a mind of that quality," so she took advantage of McClure's absence and included it in the issue. Years later she told Tarbell that when he returned, McClure said to her simply, "that story about the tramp you put in was not good enough for the Xmas number," but otherwise dropped the matter.

When Will Irwin became editor of *McClure's* in

1906, Roseboro' told him that, before O. Henry moved to New York, "he was weeks in answering even the most important query, and his letters were always posted from different points—obscure Southern or Middle Western towns." Like most of his editors and readers, she did not find out until after his death that the author she had helped make famous was writing to her from the Ohio Federal Penitentiary; he had been relying on others to forward his letters to her. Porter would publish two more stories while in prison, both as "O. Henry" and both in national magazines, "Georgia's Ruling" in *The Outlook* (June 30, 1900) and "Money Maze" in *Ainslee's* (May 1901), thereby publishing one story each year while he was in prison.

In the story:

Chalmette is a community in St. Bernard Parish to the east of New Orleans; **Algiers** is across the Mississippi River from Chalmette. O. Henry is basing his descriptions of the city on the several weeks he spent there as a fugitive, before he went to Honduras. The term **nixcumrous** (often spelled "nix come a rouse"; from the German *nichts komme heraus*, or "nothing comes of this"), was a nineteenth-century expression with various meanings. O. Henry used it in several of his stories to mean *useless*, *finished*, or *played out*. The reader will notice that Whistling Dick has a fondness for whistling tunes from operas: **Der Freischütz** is a German opera by Carl Maria von Weber that premiered in Berlin in 1821, and *Cavalleria Rusticana* is a one-act Italian opera by Pietro **Mascagni**.

A CHAPARRAL CHRISTMAS GIFT

First published in *Ainslee's* (December 1903)
Collected in *Whirligigs* (1910)

When Porter left the Ohio Penitentiary in late July 1901, he was the author of four stories and several poems that had been published in national magazines under various pen names, and he took with him the manuscripts of at least eleven stories ready for publication. One of the stories, "A Blackjack Bargainer," had already been accepted by *Munsey's*, and it appeared in the August issue. Another ten would see print during the following decade. Many of them dealt with the members of the American underworld: tramps, conmen, burglars, robbers, even murderers. As Gerald Langford (author of *Alias O. Henry*) points out, in each of these stories about criminals, "the plot invariably turns on the regeneration of an admitted delinquent, not on the vindication of a character who is blameless. Is it reading too much into the stories to interpret them as an oblique attempt at confession, even at self-abnegation?"

"A Chaparral Christmas Gift," one of his redemptive stories written in prison, appears to have been a favorite among his friends, but editors seemed hesitant to publish it. For a holiday story, it was quite violent for its time—even its "happy" ending is undercut with a violent denouement—and that may have been the reason for editors' hesitation. It finally appeared in the December 1903 issue of *Ainslee's* and proved popular, gaining even more fans when it was included in the collection *Whirligigs*, published three months after O. Henry's death. One contemporary critic compared the story to the tales of Edgar Allan Poe: "The sharp abrupt introduction, the unexpected turns of language, the rapid direct action, the sudden tragic conclusion—all these illustrate the fine quality of O. Henry's best work. Structurally, the story can hardly be improved. The method of Poe has here been turned to new uses; and its effectiveness can hardly be questioned." The story was soon adapted as two relatively successful silent films: "The Mexican's Gratitude" (1914) and the now-lost "A Christmas Revenge" (1915).

In the story:

The phrase **"herders of kine"** is O. Henry's tongue-in-cheek term for cattlemen or cowboys, *kine* being an archaic word for "cows." The retama (or, as O. Henry spells it, **ratama**, also known as Mexican paloverde and Jerusalem thorn) is a shrub-like tree commonly found in Arizona and in south and central Texas and distinctive for its dramatic clusters of yellow flowers and its ability to survive desert-like conditions.

CHRISTMAS BY INJUNCTION
First published in *The New York Sunday World*
(December 11, 1904)
Collected in *Heart of the West* (1907)

In O. Henry's America, especially New York, children seem to be always in the street. Outside a store, "coveys of ragged-plumed, hilarious children play and become candidates for the cough drops and soothing syrups that wait for them inside." Down Delancey Street, "wondering, tangle-haired, barefooted, unwashed children" gaze after a passing automobile. Elsewhere on the East Side, children "danced and ran and played in the street. Some in rags, some in clean white and beribboned . . . here the children playing in the corridors of the House of Sin." In these and other O. Henry stories, children are objects of charity, of concern, of pity, of sentimental twists in the plot—but they are only rarely full-fledged characters.

Nevertheless, a small number of O. Henry's stories feature individual children, primarily portrayed as scamps and hellions who are not quite rotten to the core. There's the ungovernable boy who torments his bungling kidnappers in "The Ransom of Red Chief." There's the mouthy young child who interrupts a thief breaking into an apartment and questions the man's competence—indeed, his very *existence*—in "Tommy's Burglar." There's the spoiled daughter of a millionaire who shows up in the last story of this collection, "Compliments of the Season." And, in "Christmas by Injunction," there's Bobby, the petulant, cigarette-smoking "brat" who agrees to act like a child for a childless mining camp if it'll get him the gift of a rifle. The children in these and a few other O. Henry stories all have something else in common: their utter dismay at the inexplicable, comical, and, yes, childish conduct of adults.

From December 3, 1903, to November 12, 1905, O.

Henry wrote one short story each week for *The New York Sunday World*; only one week's issue during this two-year marathon doesn't include one of his tales. In addition to his pieces for *The World*, he somehow managed to publish more than a dozen stories in various magazines. "Christmas by Injunction" appeared in *The World* midway during this period, and the tale is atypical among his pieces for two reasons: it's twice as long as his usual story for the newspaper and it is one of a handful set outside Manhattan. It's possible that he had written it for the higher-paying magazines and, failing to place it in time for the Christmas editions, he used it instead to fulfill his required Sunday installment.

In the story:

The setting of the story is the fictional mining town of Yellow-hammer somewhere in the American Southwest, with prospectors arriving from the **Gila country** (the region around the Gila River Valley in south-central Arizona), the **Salt River** (a tributary of the Gila River in east-central Arizona), and the **Pecos** River (extending from north-central New Mexico across Texas to the Rio Grande).

The character Baldy says he has **seen the elephant and the owl**, a nineteenth-century expression often rendered as "seen the elephant and heard the owl," meaning he has gained vast knowledge through wide and demanding experience. **Seidlitz powder** was a common laxative. **William Cullen Longfellow** is a combination of American poets William Cullen Bryant and Henry Wadsworth Longfellow. *The Swiss Family Robinson* is an 1812 novel by Johann David Wyss about a family shipwrecked in the East Indies who survive on a tropical island.

Among the games mentioned are **Chuck-a-luck**, a dice game; **"Pussy Wants a Corner"** (also called Puss in the Corner), a game in which players occupy spots in a room and at a signal try to exchange places before an additional player can reach one of the vacant spots; and **King William**, a children's kissing game in which the party sings a song beginning, "King William Was King James's Son."

THE GIFT OF THE MAGI
First published as "Gifts of the Magi" in *The New York Sunday World* (December 10, 1905)
Collected in *The Four Million* (1906)

O. Henry was a notorious procrastinator; the editors who had to deal with him filled their memoirs with what might be described as complaints wrapped in fondness. "Up to the time he last touched pencil to paper, O. Henry was never known to get a piece of work into the hands of an editor except at the last possible moment," recalled Isaac F. Marcosson, an editor at *The Saturday Evening Post*. "Upon some occasions he completely failed to meet the schedule." Similarly, Alexander Black, editor of *The New York Sunday World*, wrote in his autobiography, "The truth is that I became accustomed week in and week out to the likelihood of receiving O Henry's stories, short as they were, in propitiatory fragments; sometimes in two pieces, sometimes in three. . . . The coming of the first fragment of an O. Henry story acknowledged the reasonableness of my official anxiety, for the weekly stories in the *World* had to be illustrated, and the illustrations needed a little information about scene and characters. Often this preliminary part (on the last day of grace) held no adequate hint for the draughtsman."

The editorial aggravation was no different for O. Henry's most famous story of all. Although there are perhaps a dozen contradictory and irreconcilable versions detailing the last-minute creation of "The Gift of the Magi," the distress of the harried, unnamed staff illustrator is common to several of them. "I'll tell you what you do, Colonel," O. Henry told him, according to one account written a quarter century later.

> "Just draw a picture of a poorly furnished room, the kind you find in a boarding house or rooming house on the West Side. In the room there is only a chair or two, a chest of drawers, a bed, and a trunk. On the bed a man and a girl are sitting side by side. They are talking about Christmas. The man has a watch fob in his hand. He is playing with it while he is thinking. The girl's principal feature is the long beautiful hair that is hanging down her back. That's all I can think of now. But the story is coming."

Where the accounts diverge is who retrieved the final manuscript later that week and how they managed to get it from the recalcitrant author. *Someone*—errand boy, editor, colleague, or friend—seems to have planted himself in O. Henry's apartment for several hours until the final manuscript was completed, but the numerous claimants to that honor could populate an entirely different O. Henry story.

In the story:

In the Old Testament (1 Kings 10:1–10 and 2 Chronicles 9:1–12), the **Queen of Sheba** and her retinue visit **King Solomon** bearing gold and precious stones, much of which she gave to Solomon, and spices, which she left in quantities never seen before or afterward. "In return, King Solomon gave the queen of Sheba all she desired and asked for, besides what he had given her out of his royal bounty. Then she left and returned with her retinue to her own country."

COMPLIMENTS OF THE SEASON
First published in *Ainslee's* (December 1906)
Collected in *Strictly Business* (1910)

"There are no more Christmas stories to write," begins this story, the last true Christmas story written by O. Henry. Yet found among his papers after his death is the initial scene for an unfinished tale, which begins:

> Now, a Christmas story should be one. For a good many years the ingenious writers have been putting forth tales for the holiday numbers that employed every subtle, evasive, indirect and strategic scheme they could invent to dis-

guise the Christmas flavor. So far has this new practice been carried that nowadays when you read a story in a holiday magazine the only way you can tell it is a Christmas story is to look at the footnote which reads: ["The incidents in the above story happened on December 25th. — ED."]

There is progress in this; but it is all very sad. There are just as many real Christmas stories as ever, if we would only dig 'em up. . . .

In the story:

Bay State Gas, about which the Millionaire could not care less, was a complicated syndicate established as a trust by financier J. Edward Addicks, who through fraud, graft, and corruption created several layers of companies to sell gas to each other, thereby pumping up the price before distributing it to Boston residents. **"The Vampire"** (1897) was a famous work by British painter Philip Burne-Jones of a woman leaning over an unconscious man. **"A rag and a bone and a hank of hair"** is a line from British author Rudyard Kipling's poem, also called "The Vampire," written to accompany Burne-Jones's painting at the New Gallery Summer Exhibition in London. Between 1880 and 1914, the renowned French actor **Sarah Bernhardt** went on nine extensive American tours, performing throughout the nation to packed theaters. According to Roman historian Livy, several dozen **Sabine** women were abducted by the founding male citizens of Rome to even out the population in the city's earliest years.

O. Henry sprinkles this story liberally with arcane and obscure words, many of which can be found in most dictionaries. Terms that might be challenging to find include **cory-**

kilverty, a made-up word referring to Benjamin Sayre Cory Kilvert, a Canadian-born illustrator known in the early twentieth century for his depictions of children; **peptomanganate of iron**, a mixture given to children as a treatment for anemia; **pleasaunce**, a secluded area in a garden, especially one near a mansion; **fi'-pun notes**, British street slang for five-pound notes; and **Beloochistan**, or the region of Balochistan, currently a province of Pakistan.

The text in this book is set in 10.25 point Verdigris, a face designed by Mark van Bronkhorst in 2003 and inspired by the work of sixteenth-century artisans who created the metal punches used to produce typefaces for printing presses by meticulously carving the reverse image of a letter or character into a steel bar.

Chapter titles are set in Desire Pro, a font designed in 2013 by Charles Borges de Oliveira, who specializes in letterforms created with paint and brush. Running heads are set in Sackers Heavy, a font issued by the Monotype Design Studio.

The paper is acid-free and exceeds the requirements for permanence established by the American National Standards Institute.

Text design and composition by Gopa & Ted2, Inc., Albuquerque, NM.

Cover design by Kimberly Glyder.

Printing and Binding by Lakeside Book Company.